Breaking Magic

THE LEGACY OF ANDROVA

ALEX C. VICK

Dedication

For Cookie, the brightest star in the sky

Contents

Prologue

"What happened to you? You look terrible. It's not the sickness, is it?"

Varun shook his head. He was deathly pale. In the low light of the underground workshop, even his hair looked white. I glanced at Garrett, who frowned.

"You should have told us you were testing again," Garrett said. "We could have helped."

Garrett was exhausted. We all were. The sickness had killed so many of us. There were almost no elders left. Our parents were long gone.

The three of us had been the best magicians at the Academy. Friends and rivals. As close as brothers.

We'd been searching for a cure ever since it started. But all we'd managed to do so far was slow it down.

"I didn't need your help. I figured it out on my

own."

"You figured out what?"

His eyes gleamed.

"I can stop it. I can stop the sickness."

"*What?*" said Garrett incredulously.

"But… how?" I added. "I thought we didn't have enough magic left. All the spells we've tried lately haven't worked."

"I found a new energy source."

"Where? When?"

"How does it work? Show us!"

Garrett and I were speaking over each other in our excitement. The first hope I'd felt in months was sharp and almost painful.

"Oh, don't worry, I'll show you. We have plenty of time. We're going to live forever."

Silence. I thought I'd misheard, but his expression was ominously serious. The back of my neck prickled with a sense of foreboding.

"What did you say?" asked Garrett slowly.

"You heard me."

"But… that's more than a cure," I said. "We can't change the balance between life and death. I don't want to live forever."

"Don't you? Pity. I could have guessed you'd say that. Cal the do-gooder. Always on the side of what's *right*."

I stepped backwards. This was getting very weird, very fast.

"Look, Varun—" Garrett said, but he was interrupted.

"No. You do what *I* say now. Now and forever. Both of you. All of you!"

1 My First Gathering

The beginning of it all was completely unremarkable. My life-giver was an ordinary Breeder. I don't remember her, obviously. She was long gone before I was old enough for the first memory to stick in my head.

I'll go forward six years. I knew my place by then. The rules of Imberan society were brutal, but we could depend on them. Opta rule, Exta serve. Until our skills reached their permitted level: developed enough to be worth donating, but not powerful enough to be a threat.

Nice word that, isn't it, donating? Makes it sound like we offered our skills to a worthy cause. They were stolen, along with everything else keeping us alive.

When I was old enough, I was assigned to a unit. The Opta sorted us according to personality and skills so that each unit had a balance of each. They admire uniformity.

I suppose that's why they all look the same. White-haired, white-skinned ghosts. Not that I've ever seen a ghost. But I imagine they'd be like faded copies of real people.

My unit looked after the city's buildings. We were the lowest of the low. Repairing and cleaning. No job too degrading. And I was a Worker, not a Thinker. Which put me right at the bottom of the pile.

Before I was old enough to wonder why we allowed the Opta to treat us that way, I knew the answer. We outnumbered them ten to one, and yet they had *all* the power.

A word, that's all it took to activate the process. The Initiation Word. We didn't know what it was, and we all lived in fear of hearing it. Workers couldn't read, and we couldn't write, but we could still be afraid of that word.

It was worse for Thinkers. Reading and writing was their thing. Stumbling across the Initiation Word by accident was something that showed up in Thinker nightmares regularly.

There was a timetable according to age. We were supposed to be safe until our names appeared on the list.

But sometimes the Opta said that word as a punishment. It didn't take much to annoy them. It never made sense to me when I was younger. They were our masters, with the best of everything Imbera had to offer, and yet they were so discontented.

I didn't get it at the time, but I do now. They weren't discontented. They just wanted us to be afraid of their anger. It amused them to invent reasons to punish us.

There I was, six years old and joining my unit. I remember being excited at leaving the childstation. I was so trusting. So *stupid*. I actually believed that things might not be as bad as they seemed. That I had plenty of time to change the world before anything happened to me.

My "brother" was called Garrett. He was twelve. He'd be my brother for the next six years, until he was eighteen. Then I'd be twelve, and I'd get my own brother to look after.

"I'll call you Cal for now," he told me. "You'll have to grow into that name of yours."

He was so angry at first. His grey eyes were like storm clouds. I didn't realise he'd just lost his older brother to the Gathering. I thought it was my fault. Those first few days I carried rocks until my hands were bleeding, I was so desperate to win his approval.

"Cal," he told me, sighing with frustration. "You have to pace yourself. There's not going to be any less work tomorrow if you do more today."

He wrapped my hands in faded strips of blue

cloth torn from an old shirt. He tied the knots very tight, and I remember trying not to flinch. I didn't know it then, but he'd intended to hate me. And he wanted me to hate him too.

But I followed him around like a miniature shadow. No matter how much he scowled at me, I was determined to be friends with him. I guess I wore him down.

The brother/sister pairing system in the units wasn't just for teaching and learning. It made us care about each other. Caring made us vulnerable, and the Opta knew that. Garrett was trying to defy the system when he pushed me away.

Our unit, being buildings maintenance, was nearly all Workers. But we had an allocation of two Thinkers to help us plan our tasks more efficiently.

Life settled into a pattern of work and sleep. There were never quite enough Exta to go around, so the workload was heavy. It was deliberate. The breeding programme produced no more than the city's resources could sustain, which also happened to be slightly less than the workload required.

The sky was dark for three days out of every four. On the fourth, the red sun rose slowly in the sky, and the Opta stayed inside. We were allowed to work a shorter day.

In those precious hours, we could talk to each other without being overheard, and the future seemed less bleak. When we were feeling brave, we met up with other units and talked about what we might do if we were ever free.

"I would eat all day long and sleep in a proper bed!" I said. My young age kept my dreams simple.

"I would speak to who I want," said one of the older boys, throwing a stone away from him forcefully. Dervan had just been assigned to road repairing. Permanently. This was his punishment for striking up a forbidden conversation with a girl from another unit while they were both on cleaning duty.

I didn't get what was so great about girls then. I thought Dervan was mad. But some of the other boys nodded in understanding.

"I'd build a boat and try to find out if that shape in the water is another city," offered Talik, the oldest member of our unit. "Maybe the Opta don't live there." He was counting down the days until his eighteenth birthday, and his eyes flashed with a mixture of suppressed rage and sharp fear.

"What would you do?" I asked Garrett.

"Discover. Learn. Negotiate. Rebuild this world into something decent." Rude laughter and shouted insults greeted this. Garrett ignored them.

He became my best friend. I hero-worshipped him. I grew taller than the other boys my age, and stronger, but he never called me Callax. As long as I was Cal, we could pretend that we weren't both getting older.

In time, the boys in the unit looked up to him too. He was a natural leader. Smart enough to be a Thinker and a Worker, but that was against the rules. It was not permitted to have too many skills in one Exta. He was just a Worker, quietly doing what he could to protect the weaker boys in our unit.

We lived in the caves, when we weren't working. It was miserable. Those hours in the sunlight prevented us from being as pale as our Opta rulers, but it was never quite enough.

I always felt like chasing the sun to the distant horizon when it disappeared from the sky, hoping that it might come back if I wished hard enough. Did I mention how stupid I was back then?

The city was built on a rocky island in the middle of a giant ocean. The buildings were piled into the available space, like stone boxes. The ocean kept us trapped as much as the Opta did. Talik never got to build his boat, of course.

The years passed, and boys came and went. As long as Garrett was there, I felt like I could handle anything. Then I turned ten years old, which meant that I was required to attend the Gatherings. Two or three times a week, for the rest of my life. The reality of being an Exta hit me like a rock to the chest.

We lined up in rows in the central square, outside the ruling house. It was taller and grander than the others, extending five stories high. And that's not counting the statue.

All of the other buildings looked the same from the outside. It made our jobs a tiny bit easier. Every piece was the same size, and in the same place.

Not this one though. Rows of curling symbols surrounded the enormous doorway. What was the point of that? Decorating it didn't change what happened there.

I was scared to look at the symbols for too long in case the Initiation Word was hidden in the pattern. The statue of the great Flyer rose up from the roof, a menacing reminder of Opta authority.

It was all wings, talons, scales, and feathers, with a long spiked tail thrown in for good measure.

Every Exta was plagued with visions of these fire-breathing Flyers whenever we worked outside. They swooped across the ocean towards our island one after the other, disappearing when they reached the centre. Purple and silver, gleaming even on the dark days.

It was an unnecessary reminder that we served the Opta. If we could see the Flyers, we could not escape the process. We were told that it was a sign of our stupidity, because our weak minds were so easily led.

Garrett stood next to me, with his hand on my shoulder as a warning not to run. We were quite far back, but I could still see the victims when they crawled into the square.

I panicked at first, and Garrett's fingers dug into my shoulder. I'd known that Dervan would be there, and I'd also known that no one came back from the Gathering. But I still wasn't prepared for what I saw.

He'd left us three days earlier, summoned to be bound by the Initiation Word on his eighteenth birthday. We'd sent him off with the usual bravado.

"Some people will do anything to get out of a day's work, won't they?"

"Give the Opta one of these for me!"

This was accompanied by a jab to the stomach.

"Enjoy sleeping above ground for once! Think of us in our cave while you enjoy your comforts…"

Garrett had clasped Dervan on his upper arm. They didn't speak, but Dervan seemed to appreciate the silent support.

ALEX C VICK

Years of repairing the roads, week in week out, had made him physically strong. These days he kept his brown hair very short, and it made his eyebrows look quite fierce.

Like most of us, he had easier days and bad days, but little remained of the boy who had exchanged a few hopeful words with that girl three years before.

His expression in recent weeks had acquired a terrible patience. That was the choice he'd made. It was the only choice left to us. How to face it. We either accepted it, like Dervan, or we raged about it. But there was no point in resisting it.

The Opta would not hesitate to seek out the entire unit and bind them too. Not even the brashest rebel, or the most desperate coward, could allow themselves to be responsible for that.

The Dervan I saw that day in the square was barely a person. His physical body, on its hands and knees, was familiar, with the same dimensions and the same hair colour. There were no visible injuries.

But the face that lifted towards the two Opta leaders was a hideous parody of the boy he had been. In his eyes was the glint of insanity, the broken pieces of a mind that had been smashed.

"Please, please, please, please, please, please, please…"

He repeated the same words over and over,

until I thought I would go mad as well. He was reaching for something from *her*, the Binder, and she appeared poised to grant it, one arm extended.

She was waiting for her brother. He was the Breaker. He was in no hurry, walking in a circle around Dervan on light feet, his expression fascinated.

"I do love my work," he breathed, the cold, quiet hiss of his voice reaching his silent audience easily. While some of us were disgusted or angry, most were afraid.

There was worse to come. Dervan's younger brother, Alken, would be made to finally condemn him.

Alken had to be dragged forward. This babbling replica of the mentor who had looked after him for so long was the stuff of nightmares.

He told me later that he was too afraid to look Dervan in the eye. The guilt writhed in his stomach like a trapped Flyer for weeks afterwards.

"Your words, Exta," said the Breaker to Alken. His pale eyes glowed brighter as Alken's face twisted with revulsion. "Say them, and I will put him out of his misery."

Garrett's hand got even tighter on my shoulder, but I welcomed it. The pain was evidence that we were still connected, still normal.

"I… I can't…" Alken's expression was terrified. He suddenly looked much younger than his twelve years. He rubbed at his hair, creating brown spikes that looked as if they were standing up in fright as well.

"Come now," the Breaker mocked. "You know how this goes. Four words. *Speak.*"

There was a pause, and the senseless pleading coming from Dervan escalated. Alken whispered something. He was made to repeat it, louder and louder, until he was screaming the words, before the Breaker was satisfied.

"Please kill my brother!"

It happened quickly after that. The Binder traced a pattern on her arm, and Dervan collapsed. Her brother lifted Dervan's life essence out of his body like a multi coloured ribbon of light.

I was torn between fascination and disgust. In the end, disgust won, and I had to swallow hard to keep from throwing up my breakfast.

The symbols on the ruling house drew the light towards them like a sinister magnet. In seconds, Dervan's life essence had disappeared.

There were seven more Exta sacrificed at the Gathering that day. It lasted not quite one hour, but it was the longest hour of my life. I had seen my future. Garrett's future. And there wasn't a single thing I could do to change it.

2 Losing Garrett

Time. My enemy. My entire existence was squashed inside a spiraling clock. The more closely I looked, the faster the numbers counted down, each one taking me inexorably towards my death.

After my first Gathering, I measured out Garrett's life in hours and days, and there were never enough.

He was patient with my questions. Yes, I would have to say the same words for him that Alken said for Dervan. Yes, the Breaker insisted on the use of the word "please."

As if it weren't enough that we asked for our own deaths. Worse, we had to ask *nicely*. How hideous was that?

No, Garrett replied, no one had ever escaped. Yes, people had died trying, and so had their units. No, we didn't know what happened to the life essences. No Exta had ever seen the Time of

Assignment.

Presumably the Opta took them. Swallowed them? Inhaled them? There was no way to make *that* image less disgusting.

There were no Opta Breeders, and the childstations were for Exta only. Our knowledge of life on Imbera did not extend beyond our short lifespans, but the Opta appeared to stay the same. We changed with every year we were alive. Yet they never did. It seemed slightly creepy.

Eventually I stopped asking questions. And every day it was the same pointless routine. Eating, working, sleeping, dreaming. Especially dreaming. Of all the things I did for no purpose, that was surely the worst.

Good dreams just made the crash back to reality more awful. Bad dreams stayed with me like a crawling hand on the back of my neck.

And always the Gatherings, a never-ending cycle of degradation and death for the Exta. Waiting in my future. In Garrett's future.

I began to think that an early binding might be easier. I could break a couple of rules, get myself punished, and it would be over within a week.

I kept going because of Garrett. I owed him that. He'd seen what was waiting for him years ago. He'd requested the death of his older brother the day before he met me.

I was so mixed up. I was jealous of the dead

brother that came first. I was furious that Garrett was going to leave me. I hated that I cared about him. I resented every single useless emotion.

Eventually even Garrett wasn't enough to keep me there. I waited until I was given an indoor work assignment. I was going to insult the first Opta I came across and then accept the consequences.

Garrett, to my frustration, seemed to know. He kept looking at me, and I could sense his disappointment. It made me more determined. I went to great lengths to avoid being alone with him.

The day before my new assignment was due to start, my luck ran out. The sun was in the sky, and it gave him the free time he needed to track me down.

I was hiding in one of the caves we didn't use very much. There was no one around because only a fool would stay underground in the daylight. He took my arm and dragged me firmly behind him, away from the unit and out towards the edge of the island. I protested, but he ignored me.

My feet scrabbled at the rock, but I couldn't get my footing. I had no choice but to go along with him. Eventually we were at the edge of the island.

He pushed me in front of him and waited,

arms folded. The rocks were sharper and narrower here, and I couldn't get round him easily. Stubbornly I remained silent.

"Cal…" he said carefully.

"It's Callax," I corrected, ten years old and full of stubborn pride.

"Callax," he repeated. It sounded wrong in his voice, and I regretted making him say it. Regret. Another stupid emotion. I wouldn't be feeling anything when I was dead, and it couldn't come soon enough.

"Don't do this."

"You can't stop me. You…" The anger rose, choking off the words in my throat, and I tried to push past him.

I didn't see him do it, but he knocked my legs out from under me, and then I was in the water. The shock of the cold temperature stole the air from my chest. The current tugged at my lower body. I clawed at the rocks, trying to climb out.

"You want to die?"

His strong hands were pushing down on my shoulders, and I sank below the surface. The cold seeped inside my head, muddling my thoughts. Instinct made me kick upwards, but he held me steady. My lungs burned.

Just about when the panic took over, he let me surface. I gasped for air like one of the big flat fish the ocean units caught when they were having a lucky day.

Garrett's face was expressionless. "Why are you breathing if you want to die?" he asked.

Suddenly I was pushed under again, and this time I really struggled. *Let me up! I need to breathe!*

When he finally allowed me to resurface, I tried to escape, choking and spluttering and pushing at the hands on my shoulders.

"Your death, Callax. If you want it, it's there. Close enough to touch. All you have to do is take it."

The third time under the water, terror exploded inside my head and my chest. I thought he was actually going to kill me. I decided that I didn't want to die after all. My movements were uncoordinated, the lack of air taking its toll.

My vision started to grey out. The rocks under the water looked like they were glowing. My lungs were agony. The icy water flooded into them. Then I was hauled back onto the rock.

I rolled onto my hands and knees, coughing and throwing up and *breathing*, taking in gulps of air so sweet that I could almost taste them.

He watched me without saying a word, until I sat up and wiped my mouth. My hand was shaking slightly.

"Callax," he began.

"No… don't call me that."

"Cal then?"

I nodded, embarrassed.

His face softened very slightly. "I'm sorry, Cal. But I can't let you throw your life away. You have eight years left. The world might change by then."

"Seven and a half years." The half years were important when your life was this short. "And you only have one and a half."

"Five hundred and sixty-one days, if you want to be precise," said Garrett firmly. "And I'll make the best of every single one of them."

I hadn't known he paid such close attention. I realised that I'd never asked. All of my questions had been about me, in one way or another.

We sat next to each other, looking away from the city, towards the horizon. The sun was starting to sink downwards, turning the sky and the water blood red. A couple of Flyers showed up as black silhouettes in the distance.

"What should I do?"

"Stay alive as long as you can. Learn as much as you can."

"But what's the point of staying alive? Just to serve the ones who are going to kill us?"

He sighed. The sun was making his blond hair look like it was on fire. It was at odds with his tired expression.

We were rock and water, he and I. As different to look at as you could find. His hair yellow and straight, mine black and curly. My dark blue eyes showed every emotion, while his grey ones were like window shutters. They darkened when he was angry, but that was the only clue they ever gave to how he was feeling.

"Don't give up. I felt like you did when I saw my first Gathering. Lots of us do. I understand."

He drew up his knees and rested his chin on top of them.

"But one day things will change. It might be too late for me, but they *will* change, Cal. If you die before your time, you might miss it."

I scoffed. "They won't change. If you go through life hoping for the impossible, that just makes you crazy."

"What's wrong with a bit of hope? If you're determined to have none, I might as well push you back into the water."

I flinched away despite myself, and he laughed, but not unkindly.

"The thing about hope, Cal... it gives you a purpose. I was so angry when I first met you. I didn't see the point of living. But you wouldn't let me switch off. Looking up at me every day like you trusted me to change the world for you."

I ducked my head. I didn't want to be reminded.

"I was stupid."

"No. You were innocent. But you taught me

how to hope again. Whatever they look like, the Opta are older than us, Cal.

"No other creature on this world lives forever, and neither will they. I'm not a Thinker, and I don't know much, but I feel it in here." He pushed against his chest.

"Try it for me. Let's make our lives the best they can be. The way you used to when I first met you."

I rolled my eyes. "I'm ten now, Garrett," I said with a long-suffering sigh. "I'm not a child anymore."

He started laughing again, properly. The thing about Garrett was that for all he could be proper and serious, his laugh was incredibly infectious. I couldn't help joining in.

Somehow he made it work, though. I started to look forward to things again. There were moments when I was glad to be alive. Not many, but enough. Our whole unit was better off because of it.

Unfortunately, this only made the time go faster. I tried to ignore it, pushing the foreboding out of my head. But there came a day when it had to be faced.

Garrett was one of the oldest boys now. For a few months he was basically in charge of our unit. He knew the most, he was the strongest, and he was definitely the wisest.

But then the balance tipped.

"NearBound… NearBound…" the whispers started. When we were close to our eighteenth birthdays, we stopped being people and became NearBound.

If we had authority, we lost it. We wouldn't be around to punish anyone for disobedience, would we? If we had friends, they kept their distance. Afraid to be near in case imminent death was somehow contagious. Ashamed that their lives would continue.

It was taken for granted that we would stop working the day before. Our younger brothers were expected to look after us. To make sure we answered our summons so that the unit was safe.

Like a handover test, I suppose. I would be an older brother myself in a matter of days, after all. I was sick with fear. I didn't know if I could let Garrett go. I wanted to be angry, not scared. But I was powerless to choose my feelings.

We said our goodbyes alone. Garrett would have the usual group send-off from the rest of the unit in the morning, but I knew I didn't want to be part of that.

I didn't say much. I put all my effort into not crying like a little girl leaving the childstation. At the time, that seemed incredibly important. Later, I would curse my silence, thinking of all the things I should have said. He made me promise to stay alive and keep learning. He thanked me.

At the Gathering three days later, it was not Garrett. My smart, strong, brave older brother was gone. Broken into bits.

I found my anger then. There was a long, awful moment when I struggled to get it under control. I had to stay calm. The Breaker was quite capable of using my emotions for his own entertainment. The boy Garrett had been deserved better than that.

"Please. Kill. My. Brother." I spoke the words as evenly as I could manage. The Breaker was curious, looking me up and down. But there were a lot of Exta on the list that day, and he lost interest soon enough.

Afterwards, Garrett's body lay on the stone as if he were sleeping. It would be a little while before his physical body realised that the life essence was gone. Only then would his body finally stop breathing.

I wanted to throw myself at him and beg him to wake up. But I couldn't. He'd made me promise to stay alive. I turned my back and walked away.

3 Benedar

"But... he's a Thinker. He can't be my brother." I scowled at the childstation operator, ignoring the curious gaze of the six-year-old boy standing next to her.

I couldn't read the allocation papers on the table next to us, but the boy obviously could. He was holding a book, of all things. When we leave the childstation, we get to take one thing with us. If he had picked a book, he definitely wasn't a Worker.

"You don't get to choose. Don't you know anything?"

She looked me up and down, and I flushed. I knew that my colourful clothes pointed to my low status. The Opta dressed all in white. The better the status of the unit, the paler the colours.

Her tunic was pale yellow. She was a bit older than me, and she wore her experience like a badge of superiority. I wasn't in the habit of looking at girls. She was the first one I'd been close to since I left the childstation myself.

She was very clean, and her skin was soft. She was smaller than me. She made me notice my rough hands, and the tear in my shirt. She made me feel stupid.

"I know that you don't match a Thinker with a Worker. I've never seen it."

"Oh, well, if you've never seen it…"

She was making fun of me. Her lips curved in a smile that wasn't really a smile. My cheeks burned hotter. Her eyes were grey like Garrett's, and I suddenly hated her for being alive when he wasn't.

"You don't know what it's like outside, do you?"

I stepped closer, and her smile faded.

"The childstation is all you know. All you see. The first Gathering you go to will be your own."

I said the last words so forcefully that I nearly spat on her. She leaned away.

"Maybe we could trade information, since you think you're so clever? You tell *me* why I'm being matched with the wrong brother, and I tell *you* what you'll look like when you die."

Her eyes filled with fear. Not like Garrett's at all. Then I felt bad. She looked at me for a moment in silence.

"I don't think you're the wrong brother for me," came a high voice. I looked down in surprise, seeing the boy properly for the first time.

He had a thin, serious face, ordinary brown hair, and looked a bit shorter than average. His eyes were the most striking thing about him. They were big, dark brown, and fierce with concentration.

I glared at him. He stared back, then grinned.

"I like him, Vella," he said to the girl. "He says what he thinks. And he's got an interesting face."

The girl glanced at me. She obviously couldn't have disagreed more. I found myself wanting to laugh.

"What's your name?"

"Benedar." He stood up a bit straighter and held out his small hand. I shook it carefully.

"Are we done here?" asked the girl, obviously wanting to sneer at me some more, but too scared to actually do it. She held her pen over the allocation papers, ready to discharge my new younger brother to my care.

"We're done." I turned and walked out, leaving Benedar to trot after me.

I tried not to think about Garrett. The last time I'd seen the childstation was when he came to collect me. It felt like the hole in my chest from missing him was going to be there forever.

"What's *your* name?"

He was slightly out of breath. I was walking fast, knowing that my unit would struggle to complete its workload for the day without my contribution. It was always tough when we lost one of the older ones. I needed to get back.

"Callax," I said abruptly.

"Can I call you Cal?"

"No!"

I sped up, not looking back to see if he was keeping up with me.

We were repairing one of the buildings near the centre of the city today. The others had spent the morning preparing the stones, sizing them and making them smooth.

They had just stopped for a hasty lunch when I arrived. We hadn't lost an older brother for a while, so Benedar would be by far the smallest and youngest in the unit.

"He's not going to be much use. He's an

even smaller scrap than you were."

Albany said what everyone else was thinking. He had his arms folded, and his reddish brown hair was a mess as usual. There was a big smudge of dirt on one side of his face, hiding the freckles underneath. He looked tired and annoyed. The other boys stared at Benedar with disappointment.

Dane was the oldest now. He remained silent, his brown eyes watchful. His spiky, light brown hair looked almost grey. It was covered in rock dust.

Benedar squared his thin shoulders, but his eyes flickered with anxiety.

"Yeah, well, he's a Thinker, not a Worker, so you'll be waiting a long time for him to be *any* use," I said flatly.

"What?"

"Another Thinker? What about Jory and Zack?"

"The Thinkers are supposed to stay together. How can you be his brother if you're never in the same place?"

"We don't *need* another Thinker! How are we going to keep up with our workload now?"

I held up my hands in an attempt to stop the flood of questions. "The snippy girl at the childstation didn't exactly put herself out to explain any of that."

I reached for some dried fish and the last piece of heavy, black bread. I was about to stuff them into my mouth, when I remembered Benedar.

I was his brother now. Whatever I thought about him, he was still my responsibility. No one else in the unit was going to look after him.

Reluctantly I turned and handed him the food. My stomach growled in protest, as if it had eyes to see what I was doing.

He tore the bread in half and offered the larger piece back to me. I looked at him suspiciously.

"It was the last piece," he said earnestly. "And you need it more than me, because you're working."

I grabbed the bread. "Don't try to get on my good side, because I don't have one," I said ungraciously.

The other boys were impressed by Benedar's generosity. Giving up food was not something we did often. Usually only for birthdays. Or the night before someone answered their summons. I had tried to give Garrett my share, but he'd refused…

I didn't want to hate Benedar. It wasn't his fault.

"Hey, Callax, give the little scrap a break."

"At least he won't eat much, will he?"

"He doesn't know why he's here either."

"Yes, I do."

We all turned incredulously to face him. He stood firm under the weight of our collective gazes.

"What did they tell you then?" I asked sceptically.

He shook his head. "They didn't tell me. But I could still put the pieces together."

"You're a scrap. You can't link yet."

It was Jory. He had emerged from the back of the cave. Zack, his younger brother, wasn't with him. Zack was probably asleep. Even by Thinker standards, he was physically weak.

Jory was still one year away from his own Gathering. We hadn't expected to get another Thinker until then.

He rubbed a hand over his close cropped black hair and looked at Benedar.

"Did I hear you right? You reckon you were linking while you were in the childstation?"

Yeah, I should mention the words that Thinkers use. With them, it was all models, ideas and pieces, and how they link together.

Linking was their thing. They didn't really *do* much apart from that.

I suppose they helped us out. They told us the quickest routes to take, divided the assignments, and put our skills in the right place at the right time.

But they never picked up a hammer, or climbed a wall. Their bodies never ached with tiredness or bruises from a hard day. We had nothing in common. Even the smallest attempt at conversation usually ended in irritation, on both sides.

"I don't reckon I was. I just was."

We looked at Jory curiously to see how he'd handle this.

"Impossible," he said, folding his arms. There was a short silence.

Well, that was a bit disappointing. I was expecting a proper Thinker argument. At least a word or two that I didn't know.

Then Benedar grinned. "You must be Jory."

"How did you...?" I said before I could stop myself.

"The others referred to the Thinkers by name. Jory was said first, which means he's the oldest. And"—he looked Jory up and down—"you are rather old."

His tone was sympathetic. Jory bristled,

and I swallowed a smirk.

"Basic logic," said Jory dismissively. "Doesn't prove you can link."

"My name is Benedar," continued the small boy, looking from one face to another. "And as I said before, I know why I'm here."

We all waited. There was another grin hovering around the edges of his mouth, and I swear the scrap was enjoying the attention. How did he get to be so sure of himself?

Then he came out with a speech that no six-year-old should have been able to make.

"It's simple cause and effect. The Opta are being forced to change the balance between Thinkers and Workers. The breeding programme is malfunctioning. There are too many Thinkers.

"I'm here because there wasn't a Worker of the right age and physical skills available."

We gaped in disbelief. Not enough Workers? That wasn't possible. It was Thinkers who were in short supply. Intentionally. And even *I* could see the point of that.

"I heard the whispered conversations. I saw the evaluation forms. They even tried to convince me that I was a Worker," added Benedar, his grin breaking through.

"I failed all the Worker tests. They

accused me of failing on purpose, but that's really funny. If I failed on purpose, it automatically makes me a Thinker…"

He giggled, and unbelievably, we all smiled back at him. Jory pressed his lips together, but didn't speak.

"I know I'm not much help yet," he continued, serious now. "I'm going to learn as fast as I can. Cal… Callax is exactly what I wanted in a brother."

He looked so certain. The others stared at me. I felt a warmth in my chest, and I tried to squash it. But I think the scrap knew he'd broken through my reserve.

The idea of additional Thinkers in the Exta population was an interesting one. We decided to ask around to see if it was happening to any of the other units.

Jory choked down his hurt pride at being wrong and started asking Benedar a lot of questions. The rest of us had to leave for our assignment, so I told Benedar to stay in the caves with Jory and Zack for the afternoon. I gave Jory a threatening look that told him I expected Benedar to be looked after.

I struggled to concentrate on my work. I remembered what Garrett had said about things having to change one day. Well, this was definitely a change.

I wished so much that he could meet Benedar. I was too stupid to understand most of what Benedar and Jory had been talking about. But Garrett wasn't. I mean, he hadn't been. *Past, Callax, past. He's never coming back.*

I was dusty, exhausted, and aching when we came back. Benedar was really happy to see me, and I returned his smile before I could help myself. What harm could it do? Being horrible to him only made me feel worse anyway.

It was the middle of the three days without sunlight, which was always the worst. There was a dark day behind, and another one in front still to go.

Exta lights were battery powered. Of course, we weren't allowed to recharge them often enough, which left us in twilight a lot of the time.

The Opta used a special power that was delivered along wires and cables, from a giant battery that never ran out. Jory had told me it was powered by the sun.

Without the sun, it seemed most of our world would die. It would be freezing cold and dark, obviously. But according to Jory, there'd also be no rain.

We didn't have many plants, and we had even fewer animals, but they both needed the light and they both needed the rain.

The sun powered the water filters too. When the rainwater ran out, we couldn't drink from the ocean without it being filtered. The Opta were obsessed with using filtered water for everything.

I wished I understood it all better. Benedar, as a Thinker, would have access to the Book Rooms. Maybe I could learn something too.

I didn't realise I'd soon be learning a bit more than I bargained for.

4 Too Close For Comfort

Benedar studied hard. He soaked up knowledge like the Thinker that he was. Within six months, Jory had joined the Workers in the unit.

"You don't need three Thinkers," he argued. "I'm close to NearBound anyway, and I might as well help with the workload."

We couldn't deny that an extra pair of hands made a difference, even if Jory was useless when it came to heights and heavy weights.

I was proud of Benedar. He never talked down to us. He was the first Thinker who was really *part* of the unit. We were all very protective of him.

Even Zack came out of his shell a little bit. It turned out that he was really observant. Once he was with the rest of the unit more often, he had some great ideas about who we should be paired with to get the most done.

And his impression of Albany in a bad mood was the funniest thing I'd seen in a long time. They looked nothing alike, physically. Zack's hair was a kind of dirty blond colour, and his eyes were blue. But he got the huffing noises and the hunched shoulders just right. I don't think we'd *ever* laughed like that together before. Though he wouldn't admit it, I know that Albany enjoyed the attention too.

But the thing that really made Benedar popular was the secret system he worked out with a girl from another unit.

He met up with a Thinker called Haylen in the Book Rooms. She was just a little bit older, and they were both lonely. She was small for her age, with brown eyes and hair, just like him.

It seemed that Benedar might be right about the breeding programme. There *were* other younger Thinkers who were matched with a Worker.

I didn't like leaving Benedar alone, but there was nothing I could do about it. Even if I'd been allowed in the Book Rooms in the first place, I couldn't read, could I? Better that I did the work my skills were suited to.

Benedar and Haylen made friends. Once they realised how easy it would be to influence the location and timing of the work assignments for their two units, there was no stopping them.

The Opta kept male and female units apart as much as possible. Even talking was completely off limits once we left the childstation, as Dervan had found out to his cost.

If the Opta knew Benedar had actually made *friends* with a girl, they would have ended it. One or both of them would have found their ears ringing with the sound of the Initiation Word. You can't be friends with someone who's dead. Problem solved.

But Haylen and Benedar were Thinkers. They quickly set up a code to exchange messages. Right under the Opta's noses.

The time they found for us wasn't much. Half an hour here and there, when the paths of our two units crossed almost by accident. But those moments were startling. They were important. Life actually *improved*.

A few stolen kisses, and suddenly Albany was working twice as hard to finish on time. The older boys had something to think about that wasn't related to the Gathering, or how quickly time passed after your seventeenth birthday.

The younger boys had a reason to laugh. A different perspective on things. Someone to show off to.

As for me, I still wasn't sure about girls. I was interested in them, but I didn't really know what to do. I felt too old to be just friends with them.

Too young to kiss them. Too awkward to even look at them properly.

I tripped over my own feet. My *own* feet. I lost the ability to speak. And my cheeks went so red. All of my nervousness rushed into my face like the sun on the fourth day.

For a couple of weeks, the rest of the unit followed me around calling me "Cal-al-al." I'd been trying to talk to Haylen's older sister, and my mouth had refused to even get past the first syllable of my name. That pretty much sums up my ability to talk to girls.

Inevitably, Jory's Gathering came round more quickly than we expected or wanted. Like most Thinkers, he struggled in the end. After he was summoned, all that knowledge inside his head suddenly became like a rock that he couldn't escape.

What he didn't know about the process, he could probably guess. Us Workers knew very little by comparison.

To be fair to him, he kept it all to himself. We could hear his nightmares, even from the farthest cave, but he never burdened the rest of us. As he walked away, we could almost see the terror oozing out of him, and he looked half-way to being broken already.

He asked us to stand near the front. He knew that Zack wasn't very strong, and he thought it might help if the rest of the unit were nearby.

It was the first time since Garrett that I had been so close to the action. I didn't like it. Jory was one of the last, and he couldn't even speak properly by the time we saw him. He was like a dying animal. Desperate and mindless.

Zack appeared to be close to passing out. His agile Thinker's brain was buckling under the brute force of the words he was required to say. His body, always fragile, was shaking and shaking.

I allowed my gaze to drift upwards. I didn't think I could watch the Breaker extract another life. This close, the expressions on his face were disgusting. He obviously got a pretty big kick out of what he was doing.

I looked at the statue instead. Its mouth was open in a silent roar, neck stretched forward and eyes slanted backward. So many spiked teeth.

They told us in the childstation that a Flyer could fit a whole scrap in its mouth and snap its bones with one bite. We were scared of the Flyers long before we saw them for real.

There was a gasp from the crowd, and I froze for a second. I looked back down just in time to see the Breaker straightening up. He'd been whispering something in Zack's ear. All my muscles locked together, rigid with tension.

Zack's voice came out of nowhere.

"Nooooooooo!" he wailed, high and thin and frantic. His shaking increased. Then his face filled with an expression of such yearning that it almost hurt to watch him.

The Binder stepped disdainfully round Jory, who was still pleading incoherently for release. She lifted her sleeves higher, showing the curling symbols on her arms. They matched the pattern on the inner row above the doorway behind her.

I wanted to look away, but I was mesmerized. The symbols were glowing as if they had a life force of their own. They were sinister and beautiful at the same time.

Zack reached for her with his whole body. Like she was the answer to every dream he'd ever had. A light flared in her eyes, and he was bound. He sagged with relief, the craving momentarily subdued.

The Opta leaders enjoyed our horrified expressions. We couldn't help leaning away. As if those few inches would protect us if they decided to say the Initiation Word again.

She traced her symbols with one slender, white finger, and both Zack and Jory fell backwards. Unthinking, unseeing, their minds no longer their own.

Her brother laughed. "See how practical this is? I bind one Exta, yet I solve two problems."

I stared, too frightened even to wonder what

he was talking about. Benedar was now the only Thinker in our unit. He was seven years old. He needed me. I trembled with the desire to run.

"Problem one… this feeble creature could not push four simple words out of his mouth. An Exta who can't obey the rules of the Gathering is no use to me. Problem two… I understand that we have rather too many Thinkers in the current Exta population."

He tapped his mouth with his left forefinger. "I had considered extracting their life essences straight out of the childstation to redress the balance. But their skills are just too lacking at that age. And the joy of an appreciative audience… far better this way."

Then he added, almost casually, "The new summoning age for Thinkers will be seventeen years. Until the balance between Thinkers and Workers is corrected."

There was a stunned silence. Did that mean…? All the Thinkers who were seventeen right now… they'd been summoned? Just like that?

"Sister, we have a busy few days ahead of us. But the *allocations* we will generate…"

When the Breaker said this, the anticipation in his face was shocking. He was almost licking his lips. I could feel my heart pounding in my chest. Fear, disgust, anger. All swirling together.

"Well, don't just stand there, all of you. I need

someone to say the required four words so that I may complete the Gathering. The Time of Assignment is tomorrow."

No one moved. The prospect of being noticed by the Breaker at that moment was hardly appealing.

"I can make it sixteen years of age for the Thinkers if you prefer."

We hardly dared to breathe. Surely he wouldn't go that far?

"Still no volunteers?" he went on. "Perhaps, then, I should start with the younger ones after all..."

I took a step forward. Anything so that Benedar would not have to face this monster yet.

The Breaker regarded me with a cunning expression.

"Your brother must be a very young Thinker for you to react so obediently."

I tried to keep my face blank. It was really difficult.

"Those boys are from my unit," I said, looking at Zack and Jory. "I want to do the right thing."

He gave a bark of laughter. "The *right* thing." Then he looked at me more closely. "As if you, an Exta, could possibly know the difference between right and wrong."

The temptation to scream back at him exactly what was wrong with this whole situation rose in my throat like a trapped bird. I had to look at my feet.

"Very well. Say it."

"Please kill my brother," I recited carefully, making a silent apology to Jory at the same time.

A few seconds later, it was done. One more Exta life consumed by the rock and symbols of the ruling house. All of Jory's brilliant ideas and gentle humour, gone forever.

It was hard to stay calm. If I hadn't been worried about Benedar, I might have grabbed the Breaker by the throat, just to see if I could squeeze some of the life essence out of him before they bound me.

I was so fixated on the image of strangling our tormentor that I didn't notice Zack until he was nearly past me. The sight of his dying older brother lying on the ground next to him had broken through the Binder's trance.

He had struggled to his feet and was shuffling slowly backwards, dawning horror on his face at the realisation that it would be him lying there at the next Gathering.

A whisper of concern swept quietly through the crowd. No one was foolhardy enough to speak, but everyone wanted to remind Zack that he was bound now.

Did you think that the Binder tied us up? Chained us to the wall with knots of rope and links of metal perhaps?

No. The binding wasn't visible. We couldn't cut it off or rip it out. It was inside us, attached to our life essence. Switched on somehow by that terrifying word.

At Jory's Gathering, when I was only thirteen, I didn't know exactly how it acted. My work assignments kept me away from the city centre most of the time. I had no idea how lucky I was.

But I knew that we couldn't leave the Flyer once it had us. And sure enough, as soon as Zack stepped out of the shadow of the statue, it struck.

His face twisted, and his body went rigid. But it was the scream of pain that shocked me. Like he was being torn limb from limb. It was the worst noise I had ever heard.

The awful thing was that Zack didn't seem to realise what he had to do to make it stop. He wasn't stepping back. The Opta leaders were watching him with malicious glee. It went on and on.

There was a muffled curse from Albany, standing near the front with the rest of our unit, and he gave Zack a great shove backwards to safety. The screams gave way to gasping sobs, echoing around the silent square.

I put my hand on Zack's shoulder, wishing I had been brave enough to do what Albany had.

The Breaker put his head to one side,

considering us. "Interesting," he said. "I didn't appreciate that your Exta sensibilities extended beyond the brother/sister pairing.

"I am going to have to check what else might be happening with the synapses in those brains of yours."

I didn't know what he was talking about. But he looked interested, which usually meant bad news.

"You," he said to me, "and you"—he turned to Albany—"will stay."

We stiffened, exchanging fearful glances.

"No, no," the Breaker added with a chuckle. "Not to be bound. I want you to see what happens between now and the Gathering. And *I'm* going to watch *you*."

5 Our First Night

There was no time to speak to the others. The square emptied, everyone wanting to get away before they were pulled into this strange situation themselves. I could only imagine how the seventeen-year-old Thinkers in the crowd were feeling.

The Time of Assignment was tomorrow. It happened every two weeks. The city would light up in blues and greens until even the sky changed colour. We guessed it had something to do with the stolen lives.

The doors were all locked though. No chance for us to see inside. The house Exta knew more about it, but they never lowered themselves to talk to the likes of me. Besides, I was glad to be ignorant. I had no desire to know how you go about *allocating* a life.

It would at least give the Thinkers two nights before they had to report for the process. Two nights. Compared to the months and months they should have had, it wasn't much.

I hoped that the rest of the unit would explain things to Benedar. I was still alive, I wasn't bound, and I had to believe I could keep it that way. Otherwise I might as well try to punch that smug smile off the Breaker's face right now.

He and his sister were not particularly impressive, outside of the whole power over life and death thing. They were pale to the point of sickness, with wispy white hair that they brushed back off their thin faces and eyes that were kind of silver, kind of purple, and totally creepy.

They looked the same age as the Exta at the Gatherings. But they couldn't be. Jory said they never changed, and he'd been going to Gatherings for eight years. Why didn't they get any older?

There were no Exta who had lived more than eighteen years. Well, not that I had ever seen. We heard rumours that the good Breeders were allowed to continue for as many as three more cycles. But they were kept separate from the rest of us. And from their offspring too.

There was also talk of a few Thinkers who had been so clever in their reasoning, and so useful to the Opta, that their lives had been extended.

Of course, these were Thinkers that were part of better units than mine. The Opta didn't notice

Workers like me.

At least, not usually. Not until today.

We were put in a downstairs room with Zack. It was disappointingly bare. No home comforts for us, even if we were in the house of the most important Opta in the city.

I didn't get to see where the Opta actually lived very often. For the inside work, my unit wasn't first choice. Occasionally I repaired an interior door, or helped to clean out a house for redecoration. It always messed with my head.

Being treated like maggots on rotting fish was bad enough. But seeing close up how they lived? I never felt more worthless than when I returned to my cave after a day spent inside.

They had beds and pillows. Soft and clean. Tables and chairs with fancy dishes. Food and drink of all shapes and colours, smelling better than *anything*. Warm water to bathe in. Books and music, and the time to appreciate them.

There were little machines carrying out all kinds of useful functions. Communication, entertainment, cleaning, heating, cooking. All the things we had to do manually, if we did them at all.

This house, and this room, were built from the same grey rock as our caves, but everything was smooth and even. The walls met in straight-edged corners, and the floor was flat.

It was warm at least, which was an improvement. We looked at each other in silence. There wasn't anything different about Zack from the outside. Whatever the binding had done, it wasn't visible.

"Sorry," said Zack eventually. He looked wretched.

I shrugged, and Albany stared down at the floor. We had no words of reassurance to give.

A girl came into the room. Her hair was shiny, the same dark brown as her eyes. Her clothes were a strange mix of black and white. Black, close-fitting trousers, a white shirt, and a belt in the middle twisted with both colours. She kept her gaze turned away as she spoke to us.

"The lower two floors belong to you until your Gathering. The upper floors are forbidden. This floor is for breaking. The other is for sleeping and eating. More will join you as they are bound."

I glared at her, but she didn't turn. I knew she could see me though. Her body leaned backwards a tiny bit. She swallowed, then continued.

"I advise you to yield. Fighting the process is impossible, and you will only make your last few days worse."

"*Look* at us!" I said angrily.

"These are your best hours," she went on, as if I hadn't spoken. "Make the most of them."

She went to leave, and I grabbed her arm.

Hard. For a second our eyes met. Mine narrowed with anger. Hers widened in shock.

"Are you kidding me? That's *it?*" I challenged. She tried to pull her arm away, but I tightened my grip.

"You *are* an Exta, aren't you? Because you're behaving like one of *them*. How many times have you made that little speech? Does it get easier the more you do it?"

"*Let go of me,*" she said through gritted teeth. "It is not for you to question who I am or what I do. You don't know anything about it!"

She succeeded in wrenching her arm free, and stepped backwards to the door.

"You don't know anything about it either," I retorted. "Didn't you see what happened? I'm not bound, and neither is he." I looked at Albany. "We're being kept here as part of some little experiment. Because of our sens—sensib... or something."

She hesitated.

"You're not bound?"

"Didn't you see?" I repeated.

"No. My unit is exempt."

She was like the childstation workers then. Protected for some reason from the actual sight of the Gathering. I got why it was necessary for the childstation workers. So that they could still raise kids with hopes and dreams to keep the system going.

But why would *she* be exempt? She saw the question in my face and pressed her lips together.

"I don't have to explain myself to you," she said, looking down her nose at me. I scowled.

"No, I suppose you don't. But why wouldn't you? Aren't we on the same side?"

"Side?" she mocked. "As if this is a contest of some kind? We're nothing. Maggots don't join together in the hopes of beating the boot that squashes them."

Huh. Now I feel stupid.

Zack cleared his throat.

"She's exempt because it would be too much. Being there for the process, and then for the Gatherings too… No one can cope with both."

Albany and I stared at him as we considered that, and then I looked back at the girl.

"Is that true?"

She raised her chin without saying anything.

"I'll take that as a yes. OK, so you're exempt. Good for you. As I was saying, we're not bound. But even if we were… we deserve more from you than some cold words about making the best of it."

I felt my anger rising again. Had she spoken to Garrett like that? As if she didn't care one way or the other?

She stepped back into the room. There were

two spots of colour high on her cheekbones.

"How dare you judge me? You don't know anything! I've never seen the Gathering. But I see the process over and over. Day after day. Swap places with me and let's see how long you last!"

At least she was talking to me properly now. Like I was a person. Even if it was kind of loud.

"I would gladly *not* last," I argued, "rather than become like you. What's the point of lasting if you stop feeling anything?"

She clenched her fists and opened her mouth. But before she could reply, the Breaker appeared in the doorway behind her. She glanced over her shoulder to see what had us all staring, and froze.

There was a small smile on his thin lips.

"Are you quite well, my dear?" he asked her. "Your cheeks are rather… colourful."

"Y-yes, Breaker. I'm fine."

He raised his white eyebrows.

"S-sorry. Varun."

Varun? The Breaker had a name? And she knew him well enough to *use* it? I moved backwards without realising what I was doing, and bumped into Albany.

"Only ten minutes, and you're upsetting the status quo already," said the Breaker, looking at me. "This is going to be fascinating."

What was the status quo? And why couldn't I stop drawing attention to myself? I should have just let her leave and kept my emotions under control.

"Alanna, I wish you to tend to our quarters now. Your sister is already there, and she cannot complete the assignment without your skills."

The girl's shiny brown hair fell forwards as she bowed her head and left the room.

The Breaker (no way was *I* going to call him by his real name) remained where he was. We said nothing, which he seemed to find amusing.

"What do you feel towards your companion now?" he said to me and Albany. "Do you regret your concern?"

Zack lowered his eyes guiltily.

I didn't want to reply. All my efforts to keep Benedar safe were in danger of being ruined if I said the wrong thing now.

"Answer me. What do you feel?"

"Um... sad?" said Albany.

"Come now, you can do better than that," said the Breaker, his voice low and menacing. "You will not satisfy me with hesitant platitudes. I wish to know what you are *feeling*. That is the only reason I have spared you."

My mouth was getting drier. He kept using words I didn't understand. I had a feeling we were completely out of our depth.

"Scared," I offered truthfully.

"Better," he acknowledged with a nod. "And?"

"Powerless," added Albany, clenching his jaw together.

"Indeed," came the reply, with a small smile. "I am glad you feel powerless, because you most certainly are. That will do for now."

Then he left the room as silently as he had arrived.

We didn't know what to do with ourselves after that. It was hours before the end of the day, and we should have been working.

I worried about how our unit was going to get everything done without me and Albany. Zack's absence would hit harder tomorrow, when he wasn't there to help Benedar plan the day's assignments. Maybe Benedar could figure something out for a few days until we went back.

Suddenly I felt sick. Zack was *never* going back. These few days were all the time he had left. And I could guess that the Breaker wasn't going to do his breaking with pillows and whispers.

That girl had been right. We should make the most of these hours. I turned to the others and tried to be cheerful. We went to look at the other rooms.

There was food, there was furniture to sit and sleep on, and there were more lights than I'd ever seen in such a small space. It was almost as bright as being out in the sun.

And the food was amazing. I'd always told

myself that Opta food couldn't taste as good as it smelled. I'd been wrong.

Part of me didn't want to eat it, knowing that it was another Opta put-down. Like, hey, you're about to die, have a taste of the kind of food we've been eating all this time. Contempt hidden under a layer of golden pie crust.

But Zack was nearly smiling. He'd read about some of these dishes and couldn't wait to try them. Anyway, the pie was so good that it almost covered the bitter taste of anger at the back of my throat.

Sleeping on the bed wasn't as enjoyable as I thought it would be. The rich food churned in my stomach, and I kept dreaming about falling off. I ended up taking the covers and curling up on the stone floor.

When morning arrived, the girl reappeared. We had been awake for ages, not accustomed to sleeping late. The inactivity was starting to make me and Albany restless.

Zack stood up.

"I'm Zack," he said politely. "This is Albany and Callax. I'd like to apologise for yesterday. Thank you for the advice you gave us."

He gave her a smile. Zack, like most Thinkers, had manners and refinement built into him. No help when facing a Gathering, obviously, but handy when talking to girls.

She blinked and then tried to smile back at him. It almost looked as if it hurt her face.

"I... I'm Alanna."

"We know. Your *friend* the Breaker mentioned it."

I regretted the horrible words as soon as I'd spoken them. She blushed and then glared at me.

"He's *not* my friend," she said furiously, and then looked over her shoulder as if she thought the Breaker might be standing behind her.

"Yeah, but none of *us* are on first-name terms with our murderer."

It seemed like I wasn't going to stop saying mean things any time soon. Albany nudged me and frowned. Zack looked embarrassed.

The girl's former coldness settled back onto her face like a mask.

"The Time of Assignment is today. You're required to help me and my sister with the preparations. Follow me."

6 Assigning Life Skills

She took us underground. Most of the houses had underground rooms carved out of the rock to make use of all the available space on our little island city. Garrett once told me that the city had collected all its soil that way.

The soil was carefully looked after in the cultivation sector. There was some kind of system in place to keep it working. Like we couldn't grow stuff in it every season or something. It was nothing to do with my unit, so I didn't know very much.

We walked through a room where black-looking ocean water lapped at the floor's edge. Then we entered a tunnel, dimly lit and cold. Small droplets of water trickled down the walls.

The girl said nothing. I could hardly blame her. The only noises came from the sound of our footsteps, our breathing, and the dull jangle of keys from her belt.

At the end of the tunnel was a door, built perfectly into the rock so that there was no gap between it and the tunnel wall.

The girl extracted one of the keys and turned it in the lock. The door swung open easily. Obviously it was well maintained, though I knew that no one from my unit had ever seen it before.

The light inside was blinding compared to the dark tunnel. We all held our hands up to our eyes for a few seconds. When I was finally able to see again, all I could do was stare.

The room was enormous. Easily the biggest I'd ever seen. Like all the rooms in a house laid flat next to each other and joined together. The far wall was almost too distant to see clearly.

But it was the machines that held my gaze. They were white boxes humming with energy, stacked on top of each other. Softly glowing purple and silver letters were displayed at the front of each one.

There was a system of cables and narrow, transparent pipes snaking along the walls. I suppose the machines used the sun to keep them alive, which explained the cables. The pipes were empty though.

The girl walked up to a large machine with a big display. She took out a piece of paper and started tapping at something. The sound of her fingers hitting the machine clattered in my ears.

Zack stepped past me and began to read the displays.

"What do they say?" I asked him.

"I don't know. It's like a code or something. They're not real words."

The girl turned. She opened her mouth, and then closed it again.

"What?" I said. "What were you going to say?"

She shook her head. The expression in her eyes was like... Wait a minute. Was that *pity*?

My temper, still close to the surface, rose up and made my face feel hot. I struggled to control it. *Remember Benedar.*

"I wonder..." said Zack, almost to himself. "I wonder if these are anything to do with the Gathering? There must be a way to link..."

He moved down the row, his small fingers brushing against the displays as he passed them.

The girl was about to return to her tapping, when I marched up to her.

"What are we supposed to be helping you with? Can you at least tell us that?"

OK, now she *definitely* looked sorry for me. To my surprise, my anger retreated. It was replaced by fear. She sighed. Then she lifted her sleeve.

I shrank backwards, half expecting to see the same curling symbols that the Opta leaders had. Maybe the girl was an Opta after all, and we'd been tricked.

But her arm, although it was a lot whiter than mine, appeared to be blank. Then, leaning closer again, I saw something faint and silver-coloured.

She tilted her arm so that the nearest light cylinder shone straight at it. There was a line of letters written under her skin.

Albany peered around me to see, and I called Zack. He took one look and immediately lifted his own sleeve. His arm had the same thing.

With a feeling of dread, I checked my own arm, and the lettering was there too. I rubbed at it, but it remained stubbornly etched in place.

"You can only see it under this kind of light," said the girl, in a low voice. "Ten digits, letters and numbers, unique to each of us. Our skills are recorded against it. First when we leave the childstation and then again during the process."

Zack had gone even paler than normal. He turned to the machine closest to him and touched the display with a hand that shook.

"The life essences," he said. "They're here?"

She nodded. For a second, my vision went grey, and the floor seemed to shift under my feet. We were surrounded by the lives of the Exta. Boxes and boxes of lives. A whole room full of them.

I heard her voice again, and it sounded like she was talking from the back of a cave.

"The Breaker pushes the life essences towards

the ruling house. The symbols channel each one to the correct container.

"The programme order is set in advance, and I... I key in the codes. For receiving, like yesterday, and allocating, like today."

"That's your *job*?" said Albany incredulously. "Filing lives like they're work assignments?"

We stared at her. There was a long silence. She lowered her gaze. I glanced at Zack, worried that he was going to collapse. His whole body was shaking now, not just his hand.

He took a deep breath and clutched his upper arms in an attempt to stop them from trembling so much. He was only twelve. One year younger than me, and three years younger than Albany.

"Are you a Thinker?" he asked the girl.

What? What did that have to do with anything?

"No," she said. "There are no Thinkers in the ruling house. Just Workers. We are taught how to read the ten-digit codes, but we're not Thinkers."

Zack turned to me. "We should take this chance to learn as much as we can about what happens here."

I guess my lack of enthusiasm for that idea showed on my face, because he immediately spoke again.

"Don't you see? You and Albany will be allowed back to the unit. You can tell Benedar about it."

He gestured to the girl.

"They don't let Thinkers see any of this until they're bound. That must be deliberate. Maybe there's a weakness in the system."

"No way," I said. "I'm not giving space in my head to all the gory details! Anyway, it's too risky."

His expression became determined. "Please, Cal. You're strong. You can handle it."

He was the first person since Garrett to call me Cal. I did my best to stamp on the sadness.

But there was a small voice in my head that was reminding me of the promise I'd made. Keep learning, Garrett had said.

"Alright." I turned to Albany, and he nodded too.

Zack stood up straighter. The girl looked horrified.

"I'm not telling you everything! I have strict instructions, and he'll know if I don't follow them. He always knows, and then he'll punish me and Kaylar."

"Who's Kaylar? Your sister?" asked Zack. She nodded.

"Don't you want her to have a better life than this?" he asked.

"Of course!" she replied angrily. "But I'm not stupid. I might not be a Thinker, but I *live* alongside the Opta. I know what they're capable of."

"What are your instructions?" said Albany.

"To keep to my script. As if you were all bound, and about to start the process. And not to answer any questions."

She made a small gesture of frustration.

"You made me *talk* to you yesterday! I never do that. My sister trained me how to do this job, and for a whole year I've done it right. Until you."

She gave me an accusing look. She was my age, then. She'd been an older sister for one year.

"I can't be the only angry Exta you've had to deal with," I said defensively.

"You're the first one who hasn't been bound. Once they've had a taste of Vita's symbols, everyone is more inclined to obedience."

"Vita? Is that the Binder?"

"Yes."

I remembered the way the Binder had traced her symbols, and how Zack and Jory had collapsed. I remembered how every Exta begged her at their Gathering. I shivered. Was what the Binder did so bad?

"What does she mean?" I asked Zack. "Did it hurt that much?"

He shook his head and looked down.

"Then why…?"

"It felt good," he said quietly. "Like the best, the happiest, the most joyful feeling I've ever had. I wanted it to go on forever.

"I would… if I were offered it again right now, I don't know what I would promise to do. Probably anything."

Albany and I gaped at him. *Anything?* I didn't understand. How could anyone want happiness that much? Happiness wasn't worth dying for.

"The younger you are, the greater the effect," said the girl. "You can't help it," she told Zack.

There was almost a hint of sympathy in her voice. But maybe that was wishful thinking on my part.

"It's *his* symbols that cause the pain," she went on. "They use both to properly break you. Your life essence is hanging by a thread at the time of the Gathering. All he has to do is…"

She made a scoop out of her right palm and lifted it slightly. Albany looked like he might actually throw up on her shiny black boots. I sort of hoped he would.

"And those words he makes us say?"

I was trying to copy her detached tone of voice. Not entirely successfully.

"Unnecessary. He just likes to hear them. Gatherings for exempt units aren't done in public, and they don't use those words. But the life essences arrive in this room all the same."

"So many," said Zack, looking along the rows of boxes. "I wonder why there are so many?"

"I suppose there are a lot of Exta in this city," said Albany. "I mean, a box for everyone would be quite a lot."

"No. The Time of Assignment is every two weeks. In from the Gathering, then out to be allocated. They shouldn't need a box for everyone." He paused to think.

"Why would they need a box for everyone?" he repeated.

I wished I were smart enough to be able to answer him. I was only just keeping up with his argument. He was right though.

My box in this room could be like my sleeping place in the cave. Before I arrived, it had belonged to someone else. And it would belong to someone else again when I left. I didn't need it forever.

"Can we find out if we all have boxes?" Zack asked. "Can you check our ten digits against the records in that machine?"

Suddenly the machine made a noise. It was loud, and sounded like a warning. The girl jumped and gave a little gasp of fear.

"I'm not finished!" she whispered. She picked up a small communicator that was attached to the machine and spoke into it.

"Kaylar?"

"Yes?" came a high, young voice.

"Push the lever for the five-minute extension. I need the extra time."

"Yes, Alanna. Should I tell the Breaker?"

"No! I'll be ready. I promise."

"OK, Alanna."

The girl turned back to us. A look of concentration settled on her face, hiding the fear, and she started issuing instructions.

"Spread out. I've got five to allocate. When you see the display start flashing, press the top button. Don't hesitate. We don't have long."

We did as she asked. This was obviously not the time to mess around. She started tapping again, and the first box to react was right next to me.

I pressed the button, and the thin pipe behind it lit up with a rainbow of light.

It was unmistakably a life essence, just the same as I saw at every Gathering. I closed my eyes.

Guilt and useless anger swirled together in my chest. I couldn't watch it.

Fortunately it was done quickly. We returned to stand in front of her.

I was trying my hardest not to think about what was happening to those life essences now. No one said anything.

To my surprise, she spoke first.

"It takes an hour. They will not emerge before then. I will answer your questions."

7 The Map

"What changed your mind?" I said suspiciously.

"The questions you started asking... I want to know the answers too. And I realised that Kaylar is still too young to take over. They can't bind me yet."

We stared at her. I'm sure I wasn't the only one thinking that it was a trap.

"What?" she said, folding her arms defensively.

"You could be lying to us," I replied. "You could have been told to give us bad information. To get us to trust you and then—"

I didn't get to finish my sentence. She leaned forwards and pushed her angry face right up to me.

"I *hate* you!" she said fiercely. "You've been trouble since the moment you arrived. You're making everything different. The walls are falling down, and I can't stop *thinking!*"

I stepped backwards, but she followed me. I could see some small freckles on her nose. The more she scowled, the more scrunched up it was.

"I'm only supposed to talk to my sister and the Opta. I was *chosen* for this unit because I can build walls inside my head and keep my job trapped behind them. But you… you…"

Her eyes got wet. I had a crazy urge to laugh. Not the kind of laugh when something's funny, but when you're so nervous that you don't know what else to do.

I managed to keep my mouth shut. She managed not to cry. After a couple of deep breaths, she stepped back again.

"Your force field must be incompatible with mine or something," she muttered.

"Um, what?" I said stupidly.

"Force field," repeated Zack. He was looking at us curiously. I turned to Albany for help.

"Do you know what a force field is?"

I was relieved when he shook his head.

"It's just another word for life essence," said Zack. "The Opta's are brighter and better than ours. That's why the Initiation Word doesn't bind them."

"Do you want me to answer your questions or not?" asked the girl.

"Why would our life essences be incom… or

whatever you said?" I frowned.

She shrugged, back in control again. "I don't know why. It just happens in the pipes sometimes. When the lights won't merge for the allocation and I have to send them separately."

I made a face. "That's revolting."

"That's my job," she said flatly. "I didn't get to choose it any more than you got to choose yours."

I could hardly argue with that. And I didn't want her screaming in my face again, so I kept my mouth shut.

The three of us put our heads together and had a quick discussion. If this *was* a trap, then she was really, really good at pretending. We decided to trust her.

Zack asked the questions, and she answered them. It turned out that we all had a box with our ten digits on it. She allowed us to ask the machine where they were in the room.

Mine was right at the back. Zack said that meant I had been either first or last, depending on the order that the room had been filled.

I touched the display and couldn't help shivering—like the box contained my ghost or something, even though it was empty right now.

There were three larger boxes without codes on them. She said they were used for the other creatures whose skills were gathered and allocated from time to time.

"Other creatures?" I wondered. "You mean… *animals*?"

She nodded. "Land and sea creatures. For skills that the Exta don't possess."

She had a box too. She refused to go near it though. She'd never linked the boxes before. She'd never linked anything. Those imaginary walls inside her head were supposed to prevent it.

She was told not to make eye contact. She said the walls were stronger if she didn't see our faces. She wasn't allowed to know which code belonged to which person. Her machine didn't tell her that.

She'd never seen a life essence outside of a pipe. She didn't know how to read the skills against the codes. All she did was match the codes against a list they gave her.

And, she admitted, she *preferred* the days like today. She preferred the quiet hum of the machines in this room to the screams of the Exta while the process was operating.

"Wait until you've heard them," she said to us. "At least here, the suffering is over."

We all looked guiltily at Zack. His expression faltered slightly. Then the communicator on the side of the machine crackled into life, and we jumped half out of our skins.

It was the girl's sister, worried about what was taking her so long to return. After a few reassuring words, the girl put the communicator down and told us we only had ten more minutes.

To Zack's frustration, she wouldn't let us examine the machine ourselves. She said the risk of discovery would be too great.

Zack pleaded with her. He argued that her job was only one small part of the whole operation. The system must be divided into lots of pieces so that no one could make the links. The machine was our best chance of seeing past this room. But she wouldn't change her mind.

We were all starting to lose faith in the plan. The information we'd learned so far was only feeding our fear. It wasn't helping us understand why or how any of this was happening.

But then we had a small breakthrough. Zack spotted a folded-up piece of paper tucked behind the back of the machine. It could only be seen from a certain angle.

It turned out to be a map. A map of the pipes and how they were connected to each other. At first we thought it was just showing us the route in from the Gathering and out for the Time of Assignment. Every Opta house in the city was shown as a destination.

"Where is that?" Albany asked, pointing at a building set apart from all the others.

Zack read the words slowly. "Breeding station."

"Why would the pipes be connected to the breeding station?" I said. "Opta don't breed."

Zack peered at the map more closely.

"The pipes separate here," he said, pointing. "Just the other side of that wall, they converge into some kind of"—he looked down again—"filter, it says. Then one goes to the breeding station and the others to the city.

"I don't know exactly how or why a life essence would be filtered," he added, anticipating our question. "I mean, we filter our water to make it clean enough to drink, but that's hardly the same thing…"

"I know why. I bet the Opta get the clean part, and the breeding station gets the dirt," I said bitterly. "Just to make sure their force fields are—what did you call them? Brighter and better, wasn't it?"

"I hate to say it, but you might be right," admitted Zack.

"Time's up," said the girl abruptly. "The map is no use to anyone if we get caught," she added defensively.

I grabbed the map from Zack and folded it up small until it fit down the side of my boot. We returned upstairs, and the girl stayed with us.

"Don't you have somewhere else to be?" I said rudely. "Fluffing pillows for your friend the Breaker or something?"

Right then, she was my focus for all the bad feelings I had about our recent discoveries.

"Cal," said Albany. "Callax," he corrected himself when I glowered at him. "Don't be an idiot. She's only doing her job."

"I don't want to stay with you," she said. "But I have to. He's going to question us all."

I was wondering if I could blame her for that as well, when the Breaker appeared. He had the Binder with him.

They looked sharp and dangerous. Their eyes were glittering. The Time of Assignment agreed with them.

He did all the talking. Question after question, until it was hard to remember everything I'd said. I was scared that I was contradicting myself. Why was my brain so slow?

Fortunately he concentrated on our emotions, rather than what we had been doing. The worst thing was that he insisted we use his name. It was obviously important to him.

"Alanna can tell you that the process works much better for me when we use our chosen names," he said.

Better for *him*? The rage inside me wanted to explode in a roar of frustration. I nearly choked on it. His superior expression seemed to say that he knew exactly how I was feeling.

He hesitated when he got to my name.

"Cal…" he said slowly. "Cal."

"Callax," I said, before I could help myself.

"Only Cal to your friends?"

I gritted my teeth.

"You will answer me," he said. His voice was soft, but the threat was clear.

"Only Cal to… to… my brother."

"And his name was?"

I hated this. I did not want to answer. It felt like he was stabbing my chest with a knife every time he opened his mouth.

"Garrett."

There was a flicker in his eyes. Then he turned to the Binder. "Cal and Garrett," he said to her. They seemed to find this very amusing.

"No matter the random instructions given to the breeding programme, there is a reassuring pattern to life," he said to me. "If only you could live long enough to appreciate it."

With that, they left us. The girl made to leave as well, but I stopped her.

"I'm sorry, Alanna," I said. She blinked. "I am," I continued. "Spending time with him is like a living nightmare. And you do it every day. Even if I don't like you, I kind of admire you."

She looked at me as if I had two heads.

"Don't expect me to bend down and kiss your feet just because you said sorry," she retorted.

"Kiss my feet?" I repeated. I scrunched up my

toes in their dusty brown boots. She blushed bright red. Zack and Albany grinned at each other.

"I don't want *anything* from you," I said nervously.

"Good, because you're not getting it!"

"Good, because I don't want it!"

Zack giggled and I glared at him. Alanna marched out, her nose in the air.

The others looked at me.

"What?" I said belligerently.

Albany smirked. "I suppose it's an improvement on Cal-al-al," he said.

I smiled reluctantly. I suppose it was.

Once again we didn't know what to do with ourselves. We ate some more food, even though we weren't really hungry. We'd eaten more food in the last few hours than we usually ate in a week.

As the day went on, Zack began to get scared. Albany and I tried to distract him, but we weren't very good at it.

We all pretended to sleep, though I know the others were just as wide awake as I was. Early in the morning, the seventeen-year-old Thinkers started to arrive in answer to their summons.

There were so many. I couldn't really count much past ten, so I didn't know for sure, but it was somewhere in between one lot of ten and two lots of ten.

Albany and I were sent to wait underground with Alanna and her sister. I was sorry to leave Zack on his own, because he was by far the youngest. But I didn't want to hear the Initiation Word.

Kaylar was tiny. She darted from place to place like a small black-and-white butterfly. Their room was definitely better than our cave. It had light from a cable, and blankets too.

Alanna made a point of telling us that her sister didn't know everything yet.

"She hears the process from down here, and she helps with the Time of Assignment, but that's all. You can't tell her what you saw yesterday. Not until she knows how to imagine a bigger wall to keep it all behind," she said fiercely.

Kaylar looked at me.

"Will he destroy *my* walls too?" she asked Alanna curiously.

"No," replied Alanna, giving me a stony look. "He'll be dead by then."

"So will you," I snapped back.

"What happens next?" asked Albany. "How long do we have to wait?"

"She binds them. She uses her symbols, and they surrender. Some will try to fight it, but none will succeed. By the time we see them, they will all be wondering when they can have her symbols again."

Her voice was expressionless.

"Her symbols will be repeated before we sleep. In the morning, their force fields will be softer and weaker. His symbols will tear into them like a…"

She looked at Kaylar. "Like something that hurts," she said carefully. "Something that hurts a lot. They will tell him whatever he wants to know. Then her symbols again. The force field starts to disconnect."

She paused. Her jaw was rigid with tension.

"They will be only copies of themselves. They will have no thought or will of their own. They forget to eat and drink.

"They become weak. You cannot talk to them. They will answer like machines.

"Some might recover before his symbols are used again. Most will not. He uses them anyway. He likes to be sure that they have told him everything."

She clenched her hands in her lap, but her voice remained calm.

"Then her symbols again. This is usually enough to break them completely. Their only wish is to have her symbols. They beg and beg and beg for them. All day and all night. Then the Gathering."

She lifted her eyes to mine.

"And you know what happens at the Gathering, don't you, Callax?"

8 Breaking

I glared at her. "Yes I do, thank you, *Alanna.*"

"What happens at the Gathering?" asked Kaylar.

"You don't need to know that," responded Alanna gently, brushing the smaller girl's hair back from her forehead.

Then she gave me a warning look, and I shook my head. I wasn't a monster. If Kaylar spent her days listening to the screams of torture from the rooms above her, she had enough to deal with.

Benedar's life was easy by comparison. I hesitated. Did that mean that *my* life had been easy compared to Alanna's? I'd been behaving as if she owed me an apology or something.

Not knowing how to deal with that thought, I turned my mind back to Benedar. He was still so little. Albany's brother, Sorvan, was two years older, and a Worker. The separation would not be as bad for either of them.

I paced up and down, wondering what was happening upstairs. The sound of my boots hitting the floor was reassuringly solid and I soon had a rhythm going. Ten steps to the wall, and ten steps back.

"Will you *stop*? You're making my head hurt," complained Alanna after a few minutes.

OK, maybe not everyone found it as reassuring as I did. Although I was starting to think that she would complain about me no matter what I did.

By the time we were allowed back upstairs, we were all glad to leave. We were confronted with a small crowd of dazed and terrified Thinkers.

The Binder's symbols had muddled their clever brains with waves of imitation happiness. Like Zack, they wanted it again. They were scared at how much they wanted it. There was no logic, no reasoning, that would save them.

Any small hope I might have had that the binding wouldn't work on so many at once was quickly dashed.

Zack was struggling to focus. It was his second time with her symbols. His binding, taking place at the Gathering of his older brother, was not exactly typical.

Alanna was surprisingly kind to him. She encouraged him to eat and drink something, saying that it would help him recover more quickly.

"Where are they?" I asked her in a low voice.

"The Opta elders always meet after the binding to agree how the process will work. The mix of expected skills is a bit different every time. And this time, it's *really* different."

"The Opta elders? Who are they?"

"Fifteen Opta, including the Binder and the Breaker. They make all the decisions for the running of the city. *He's* in charge, though. He's always in charge."

I didn't need to ask who she meant.

Albany and I split up, talking to as many Thinkers as we could. Normally I would have been massively intimidated, but just then I was too concerned with collecting information.

Alanna stayed with Zack, watching our conversations. She stared at all the different faces with an expression that was half scared and half fascinated. I suppose she'd never looked before.

We learned more than we'd expected to. The Thinkers were happy to talk to us. Slightly confused from the symbols and still angry at their early summons, they weren't inclined to hold back.

I confirmed that there was a pipe to the breeding station. I spoke to a Thinker who had been assigned to a unit that did pipe and cable maintenance.

Some of the skills were obviously recycled then. Probably whichever ones the Opta didn't want.

Frustratingly, no one knew why there would be more Thinkers than Workers being born. Some of the Thinkers hadn't even heard that it was happening until the Breaker told everyone two days ago.

We found one Thinker who worked on another machine like the one Alanna used. He was based in a unit made up entirely of Thinkers, in an underground hub on the outskirts of the city.

He updated skills according to the childstation test results. He used them to match brother and sister pairings. He didn't know any names, only the ten-digit codes. After the pairing, his involvement ceased.

It was like Zack had said: each unit only saw pieces of the system. No one was in a position to link them together. Maybe we could change that. Maybe.

The following day, my hopes were destroyed, one scream of agony at a time. He made us watch. Me and Albany. He tortured a roomful of people for most of the day, and we weren't allowed to do anything except watch and listen.

Just as the Binder had done, he traced his symbols one at a time, varying the pattern and the pressure according to the response he was getting.

As he asked his questions, the Binder ticked off the skills against the original childstation records, making changes where necessary.

Some of them tried to fight it. Some of them begged for our help. Some of them lost their reason right in front of me. I could almost see the threads of sanity fraying behind their eyes.

Zack was so brave. He hardly made a sound, but his tears fell in a never-ending stream. An ugly grimace of pain added years to his face.

I closed my eyes once, wishing that I could close my ears too. Almost immediately I felt a cold, dry hand on my arm, and my eyes flew open again.

"Cal?" said the Breaker, an imitation of concern on his face. "Are you feeling alright?"

It was almost the last straw. My head felt like it was being squeezed by a vice. Benedar, I reminded myself.

Unbelievably, the Breaker stopped the entire process to question me and Albany about what we were feeling. I could sense the eyes of the Thinkers staring at me. They must have hated us. Talking about our emotions while their actual life essences were being ripped apart.

Even though I knew it would take them all one step closer to broken, I was glad when her

ALEX C VICK

symbols took over. At least they could be at peace for a little while.

But it didn't get much better. Alanna had said they would be like copies of themselves. I hadn't realised how eerie this would be. Their voices were flat. Their eyes were blank. The Breaker continued his questioning. They were like his puppets.

I held my breath when he got to Zack. If he asked Zack anything about the Time of Assignment, we were done for. But he concentrated on our unit and how it operated.

I had just started breathing again when the Breaker checked his list and asked if our unit's young Thinker could cope after Zack's Gathering. In a monotone, Zack started talking about Benedar.

I knew a moment of blind panic. What if Zack mentioned Haylen? What if he described the secret meetings?

But it seemed that the Breaker's intention was not to uncover forbidden activities. He was more concerned with watching my reaction whenever Benedar's name was spoken.

I tried so hard to stay calm. The more time I spent under the Breaker's gaze, the more unsettled I was becoming. If I didn't know better, I would say it was like *recognition*.

Have you ever had a nightmare that happens

over and over? So that when it starts again on another night, you feel a creeping sense of dread, because you know how it's going to go? It was kind of like that. I didn't know him, and I didn't want to know him, but it felt like I did.

When Alanna rejoined us at the end of the day, she said nothing. I was very grateful for her silence. She must have known that we had barely survived our first day. She could have shouted "I told you so," at the top of her voice, and she would have been in the right.

She had lived alongside the process ever since she left the childstation. She had faced it again and again. And yet I had yelled at her when she refused to look at us. I had judged her without knowing her reasons. I felt pretty bad about myself.

"The Gathering will be the day after tomorrow," she said eventually. "You should try to get some sleep tonight. Tomorrow night they will be frantic. The craving for her symbols will take over completely."

I closed my mind to the thought. I'd seen it for a few moments at a time, one Exta at a time, during the Gatherings. But so many all at once, for hours and hours? No. It was just too horrible to imagine.

After a long time, I did manage to get to sleep. But the Breaker showed up in my nightmares. He was carrying out the process on me. I was screaming at him to stop. And I was calling him Varun. As if I knew him. I woke up gasping for breath.

Albany's hand was on my arm, and it was a second or two before I could hear his voice over the roaring inside my head.

"Cal...Cal... It's OK, it's just a dream. It's just a dream, Cal."

I wanted to grab onto him as if he were a boat that could save me from drowning. I tried to focus.

"H-how many times have I told y-you," I said, my breathing still uneven, "to call me Callax?"

He grinned. "Give it up, Cal. You don't want the Breaker to be the only one who calls you Cal, do you?"

He was right. It suddenly seemed ridiculous. My memories of Garrett wouldn't be ruined if everyone called me Cal.

Neither of us went back to sleep. The following day was just as bad. Knowing what to expect didn't make it any easier. Only one Thinker had recovered enough to emerge from the trance overnight. The Breaker looked disappointed.

I suppose he wanted more frightened faces. I was glad he didn't get them. It was one small crumb of comfort. I didn't feel glad for long though.

He hurt them again and again. I knew that he had to make sure they would break when the Binder used her symbols for the last time. But I couldn't believe that it was necessary for him to make it last for so long.

And he enjoyed it. Oh, he *loved* it. The pleasure he displayed at the Gatherings was nothing compared to this. This was where he really had his fun.

Every time I tried to look away, he seemed to know, and he would be at my side in an instant, searching my face for clues to what I was feeling. It was getting harder and harder to keep still.

My eyes were always my weakness. Even when I kept my expression calm, my emotions still had a tendency to escape into my eyes and announce themselves to anyone paying attention.

Zack had told me what "sensibilities" were. They included everything to do with our emotional responses, our awareness of others, and how open we were to things.

Why that would interest the Breaker, I didn't know. But some instinct told me to show him as little as possible. If he believed everything was the way it was supposed to be, then he wouldn't be paying close attention.

I risked a look at Albany and wondered how he was remaining so calm. Then I saw that his left hand was clenched into a fist at his side. His jagged Worker fingernails were digging into his palm, and fat droplets of bright red blood were dripping onto the stone floor.

This time the Binder's symbols only quietened them for a few hours. As the night went on, the desperate pleas became more and more jumbled together. Albany and I tried to comfort Zack, but he didn't even know who we were.

The Gathering was merciful after that. We only saw Alanna for a few moments when the night finally ended. She was too busy to talk to us for long.

She had received her instructions to make sure that the life essences were directed to the right boxes in the right order. There were a lot more codes than for a normal Gathering.

I knew I would probably never see her again. I wanted to say something, to tell her that I regretted almost everything I'd said to her before. But the words wouldn't come.

Albany thanked her, and she gave him a half-smile. I tried to thank her as well, and she gave me a cool look.

"Which is your birth season?" she asked me.

"Growing," I replied.

"Mine is Harvesting," she said. "I am younger than you. I will see you when you return."

Her tone of voice gave me no clue about

whether she saw this as a good thing or a bad thing.

After the Gathering, the Breaker released us. He said he was satisfied that our emotions were within normal parameters. Normal sounded good. It sounded like he was going to leave us alone.

Albany and I walked home in silence. We were both relieved beyond measure that the Breaker had not made us stay for the disposals.

I wondered how the Binder and the Breaker had learned their skills. Mine were so narrow. So small. I could repair buildings. I was physically strong. But I had nothing compared to them.

They could bind me with one word. They could tear at the force field inside me until it broke. They could steal it for themselves, leaving my body to fall down like a set of old clothes. And they could do the same thing to everyone I ever cared about.

I thought I'd seen my future at Dervan's Gathering. But I'd only seen the very ending. The binding and breaking process that must come before it would be part of my nightmares for the rest of my life.

9 What Flyers Are Made Of

Life settled back into the same pattern. We missed Jory, and we missed Zack, but we were accustomed to losing our friends. We carried on.

I knew that Dane was watching me and Albany closely when we first got back. As the oldest, he carried the responsibility of keeping the unit functioning.

He collected the work assignments from the city centre, and he made sure that Benedar kept the unit's records up to date. He wasn't quite the strongest. Not with Albany around. But he was experienced, and fast.

Being the oldest didn't automatically make someone a leader. But it was a head start, and as long as that person had half a brain, the younger brothers would look up to him.

He never said much, that wasn't his way. But I could feel his gaze on my back, and several times I turned round to find his eyes looking in my direction.

I challenged him once.

"What are you staring at?"

He thought before answering.

"You."

I laughed, and he gave me a small smile.

"That's not what I meant," I said.

"Then what did you mean?"

I considered.

"I suppose I meant *why* are you staring at me?"

He shrugged.

"You lost it after your first Gathering. I wanted to make sure it didn't happen again."

"No," I said, remembering. "It's the opposite this time."

I found that I had a new appreciation for ordinary life. When my shoulders ached from hammering rocks all day, I no longer minded.

When I woke up starving, to be faced with only a small handful of wrinkled berries for breakfast, I didn't care.

The only thing that mattered was that my mind and body still belonged to me. I wasn't bound. Every day was a gift.

Albany and I told the others what we had found out. We refused to share the details of the process. But we explained everything else.

Benedar was captivated. He made endless notes and lists, scribbling and crossing out and scribbling again. To him, the idea of a life essence in a pipe was like a fascinating story.

He'd never been to a Gathering, or lost an older brother. He didn't think of the rainbow of light as a real person.

I suppose that was a good thing. We were all hopeful that he might be able to link some of the information together.

He started sharing some of the details with Haylen. They were able to convince three of the older Thinkers in the Book Rooms to join them in their hunt for clues.

Before this, we could have searched the entire city and not found a single Exta willing to risk breaking the rules. But any Thinker who was older than sixteen had a pretty different take on life right now. They hadn't counted on being NearBound for a long time yet.

The Thinkers that Benedar and Haylen recruited were quite cynical. They didn't believe we had *any* chance of learning enough to change the whole Opta versus Exta situation. But they were glad to oppose the system while they still had the chance.

We started to build channels of communication, hidden behind small changes in work location and assignment. It was a bit like a fishing net, covering the city with fine threads that connected one unit to another.

It was frustratingly slow. Little pieces of information came one at a time, and it was all random. Benedar created a chart, showing the life of an Exta from breeding station to Gathering. But it had a lot of gaps.

There was another chart for the life of an Opta, and that was nearly empty. All we knew was that they spent their days doing as little as possible, surrounded by luxury.

What we really wanted to know was what they did during the Time of Assignment. And our chances of finding out appeared to be zero.

For that one hour, the city gave off a light far brighter than the low, red sun could ever create. It was blue and green, silver and gold, beautiful and creepy at the same time.

All the house Exta locked the doors while it was happening. Then they were required to stay underground. They were so well trained in this behavior that when we suggested they might go back upstairs to take a look, they turned white with fear.

I didn't know what punishment could possibly be worse than being bound. But we heard about brother and sister separations, along with physical penalties like whipping and starvation.

And all this time I'd thought that my life was worse than most everyone else's.

When I turned fourteen, I decided that I

wanted to learn how to read. I was fed up with relying on Benedar to translate everything for me.

He tried to teach me, but it was like my brain didn't know what to do with the letters. I couldn't remember them from one day to the next, and I definitely couldn't join them together.

"I don't get it, Cal," Benedar said to me. I was staring at the wall of the cave, my face red with embarrassment. I'd just completely failed to recognise even my own name in a sentence that Benedar had written.

"You're really smart," he added. "You should be able to do this."

Yeah. I should be able to. Not because I'm smart, but because it's basic stuff.

Benedar was still the smallest and youngest in our unit. We hadn't had a Gathering since Zack. It seemed crazy that I had ever worried how Benedar would cope as the only Thinker.

He shocked me into silence sometimes with the speed and power of his reasoning. It was like his skills were connected to the cables supplying the Opta's lights and machines.

We continued to meet up with Haylen's unit, and sometimes the units of the other Thinkers that were part of our secret operation. There were two left. One of the original three had turned seventeen since we started.

To my surprise, I found that I could talk to

girls quite easily now. And they seemed to like me, which made no sense at all.

I didn't have Albany's self-confidence. I didn't have Alken's sense of humour. My features weren't arranged perfectly or anything like that. It was a mystery.

One day I heard Benedar and Haylen discussing it, and I stopped to listen, curious about what they would say.

"I don't know either," said Haylen, her high voice carrying easily to the shadows where I was standing. "I can only tell you what my sister said."

"Go on then," replied Benedar. "Because I've applied logic to it, and I can't link their behaviour towards Cal with Cal himself. *I* think Cal's great," he added loyally. "But if I described him on paper, it would not make sense."

I smiled to hear my younger brother defending me even though his Thinker's brain had been unable to give him an answer.

"There are two things," said Haylen. "His eyes and the fact that he keeps his distance."

"His *eyes?*" repeated Benedar.

"My sister says they are the same dark blue as the ocean and that she feels like she could drown in them."

Benedar started giggling, and Haylen joined in. I frowned in surprise. My eyes were terrible. They always showed exactly what I was thinking. It was a big problem, especially when I was near the Opta.

"And his distance?" said Benedar, through his laughter. "If he is unapproachable, surely that is off-putting rather than attractive?"

"They say it's a killer combination. Him being all distant, and his eyes being so..." She started giggling again. "So watery!"

I left them to their laughter. The prospect of ever looking Haylen's sister in the face again made me squirm.

Eyes you could drown in? If the other boys in the unit ever found out, I would never live it down. Every time I blinked they'd probably start pretending to swim away from me.

And I wasn't deliberately distant. I thought I was perfectly polite. Conversation with girls was far from the stuttering disaster it had been a year ago.

There wasn't one girl that I liked more than the others though. Something always held me back from making that choice.

If I was being totally honest with myself, some*one* always held me back. She had shiny brown hair, she was brave and clever, and she had more attitude than the rest of my unit put together. Oh, and she hated me.

I wouldn't meet her again until I was

summoned. Our fishing net of information threads had didn't reach as far as the ruling house, and probably never would. It was just too dangerous.

I was resigned to the fact that I wouldn't live long enough to see our efforts amount to anything. We had to balance the speed of progress with the risk of discovery. But I was hopeful for Benedar. He would have another five years left to him after my Gathering.

Compared to where we had started from, we knew a lot. We had numbers of births and Gatherings per season, which had always been perfectly balanced. Until the recent spate of Thinkers being summoned, that is.

We knew the number of units and what they did. We knew how many Opta there were. We had a map of the city, overlaid with the map of the pipes and cables that I had stolen from the ruling house.

But there was also a lot we didn't know. How the breeding system worked, for example. The breeding station was as inaccessible as the ruling house. Once an Exta went into it from the childstation, they were never seen again.

We had a hazy idea that baby Exta were grown inside Breeders, and that Breeders had to be girls. The Thinkers argued that you must need both boys and girls to make babies. Otherwise there would be no need for both to keep being born.

I agreed with that. All the jobs that the units did could be done by either boys or girls. Our skills were never identical, but overall there was little difference.

Don't get me wrong, I liked having girls around. It was more than a year since we had started meeting Haylen's unit, and I couldn't imagine going back to how things were before.

But if I considered it carefully, the girls could probably run the city without us the same as we could run it without them. If we had to.

We spent ages discussing the pipe into the breeding station from the ruling house. It must go to the Breeders. Exta births were recorded every two weeks, and the Time of Assignment was every two weeks. But what was it *for*?

Lately we had tried to record the pattern made by the Flyers across the ocean, but it was different for everyone. I could be standing right next to another person, and they'd be seeing a different vision than I was.

All of the Flyers ended up at the ruling house. They merged with the stone in a horrible copy of the way the life essences were swallowed up at the Gatherings, showing us the way to our life's end. As if we were in any doubt about *that*.

Benedar concluded that the Flyers had to be made from energy. Like a force field without a physical form. It was hard to believe. The Flyers appeared very real. If ever I was working on the top of a building in the city, I still tended to duck when they got too close.

I wasn't the only one who had trouble believing it. We decided to put it to the test. The next day that the sun rose slowly in the sky, a few of us gathered at the rocks by the edge of the water. Right at the far end of our island.

Even if the sun hadn't been visible, the Opta never went here. It was bare and ugly.

I volunteered to do it, glad of the chance to make a proper contribution. Reading, writing, and linking were beyond me, but this I could do.

Not that it wasn't scary, balancing on the tallest rock, waiting for one of the Flyers to swoop overhead so I could launch myself into the air to try to touch it. I trusted Benedar, otherwise I wouldn't have been doing it.

I lost my nerve on the first one. Flames burst from its open mouth in a blaze of red and orange a few seconds before it passed me. I wobbled and nearly fell off the rock.

The others shouted insults, telling me that I should return to the childstation for a lesson in how to stand up properly. I gritted my teeth and waited for the next Flyer to approach.

This time I didn't hesitate. I could see its wings fan out to reduce its speed, and I threw myself off the rock and up into the air as high as I could get.

I saw a flash of talons and teeth. My outstretched hand cut right through its stomach, purple scales and all. But there was nothing there. Just a faint buzzing against my palm. It felt... odd. I almost had a word for it, and then I started falling.

I landed in the ocean with an enormous, painful splash, gasping at the cold. My head went under before I remembered to kick upwards. As the icy water hit my face, the word came back.

Spell. The Flyer was a spell.

10 Blood And Nightmares

Benedar said that the word did not exist. He checked carefully in the Book Rooms, but could find nothing like it written down anywhere.

I knew everyone thought I'd lost it when I came face to stomach with the Flyer. They told me that the word was something I'd just made up. Stubbornly, I refused to back down. The word was real.

It hovered at the edge of my mind, hinting at something really important, if only I could remember what it was. Spell, spell, spell.

One evening, after we'd eaten our small meal of fish and bitter, black grains, I went to sit apart from the others. Leaning against the cave wall, I drew my knees up and closed my eyes. I was hopeful that I might get a few moments alone before we settled in for the night.

My nightmares had returned with a vengeance since I'd touched the Flyer. I was exhausted. I craved sleep, but I was too afraid to lie down in case the Breaker's face returned to torture me. I was embarrassed because my screams usually woke everyone else up as well.

I felt someone small sit down next to me. It was Benedar. His large eyes were even larger with worry. I could see that he wanted to challenge me, but didn't know how to begin. It wasn't permitted to question your older brother. At least, not according to the way things usually functioned.

It was a bit different for me and Benedar. With him being a Thinker, and me being a Worker, he could probably question me every five minutes if he put his clever mind to it. He never had, though. Right from the start he had treated me as if I were the perfect older brother.

"I know you think I'm mistaken," I said tiredly. "Just like everyone else does. We have proof that the Flyers aren't real, and they're all happy to believe in your force field idea."

I frowned, looking down at the hand that had touched the Flyer. I was so tired that it almost felt like my head was floating. The memory of the buzzing feeling crept back. It increased in intensity until I had to scratch my palm.

Suddenly the word reappeared. I lifted my head.

"Get me something to write with," I said

abruptly.

Benedar gaped at me.

"What?" he said.

"Something to write with. Quickly!"

He scrambled to his feet and was back almost immediately with paper and pen. I understood his hesitation. I didn't know how to read, and I didn't know how to write, so what did I think I was doing?

I wasn't sure myself. But I picked up the pen anyway, and held it to the paper. The word flowed from my hand as if I had written it a million times.

Spell

Benedar was speechless.

I looked down at what I'd written. "Spell," I repeated. "A way to control or enchant using magic."

Silence. I had no idea where those words had just come from. But for a few seconds, they had smashed through the Worker fog in my brain and made me feel like a different person.

Benedar grabbed the paper and pen and hastily wrote down what I'd said. He looked at me, excited and scared.

"Cal, that's three words I don't know. Spell,

enchant, and magic."

I stared back at him. Frustratingly, my moment of clarity was fading away, and the letters on the page had returned to their customary jumble of meaningless shapes.

"Say them again," I asked him.

"Spell. Enchant. Magic."

I nodded, feeling reassured that I wasn't going to forget them.

"Don't tell the others. I want to try to understand this on my own first."

He agreed. He was supposed to do what I told him anyway, but I hoped that he saw my reasons.

Half of the unit would make fun of me. The other half would see it as further proof of my craziness. It would be a whole lot of background noise that I didn't need.

"The way you constructed your sentence... spell and magic are connected, and they are *things*," offered Benedar. "Enchant is something they *do*. Alongside control. Maybe enchant and control are similar."

"Maybe they are." I sat up straighter. "Which means that the Flyers are a means of controlling us."

Benedar grinned. "That's a link," he said. "You just made a link."

He looked proud. I reached out and ruffled his hair to hide my embarrassment.

"Don't patronise me, you little scrap," I said affectionately.

"I'm not a scrap!" he argued. "I left the childstation over two years ago."

"You're still pretty small," I said with a grin. He tried to punch me, and I held him off easily, tickling him under the ribs. Eventually he gave in and started laughing as well.

"What's so funny?" asked Albany. We hadn't noticed him walk up to us. He looked relieved to see me smiling.

"Nothing," I answered. "Just dealing with a scrap who's making trouble for himself."

Benedar gave a yelp of protest and tried to punch me again. He caught me off guard, and his small fist landed right on the edge of my jaw.

The momentum pushed me back until my head crunched against the rock. I felt something slice into me.

His eyes widened.

"I'm sorry, Cal!"

I winced and put my hand gingerly underneath my hair. It came away covered in sticky red blood. Even though I was sitting down, I felt the floor tilt underneath me.

"Go and find a medical unit," Benedar said to Albany.

"No," I protested automatically. If I got sick or injured, my chances of an early binding went up massively.

"It looks bad," Albany said.

Benedar leaned over me to look at the cave wall.

"There's a sharp bit sticking out right where your head landed. Can I have a closer look?"

I started to shake my head, but the movement made everything spin around me, and I had to put both hands down to steady myself.

Benedar gave me a gentle push, until I was lying down on the floor. I felt the shock of the cold, damp rock against my cheek. I closed my eyes, but that made the spinning worse, so I opened them again.

"Bring the light closer," said Benedar. His small hands pushed my hair to one side and he gasped.

"What is it?" I said, struggling to form the words. Everything seemed to be slowing down.

"Cal, we have to get the medical unit."

Albany's voice was coming from a long way away.

"N-no," I managed. "He'll find out. He'll come for me."

"Who?"

"Varun."

"Who?"

Benedar's voice this time. The light was fading.

"Please… don't let him get me. N-not yet…"

I closed my eyes.

My nightmares dragged me away from Benedar and Albany and kept me prisoner. I couldn't escape him. The Breaker. Using his symbols with increasing excitement. Watching me scream, and laughing triumphantly.

Whenever the nightmare started again, it took me by surprise. It was like I was expecting to be able to resist the process, and the realisation that I couldn't was terrifying each time.

The pain, and the fear, and his crazed laughter, repeated in a never-ending loop. Sometimes I heard my name being called from the shadows by someone promising safety, but I could never reach them.

And Garrett. He was there too. As trapped as I was. I'd wanted so much to see him again, but not like this. I tried to help him, but he broke in front of me.

"Cal, Cal, Cal," said Varun, shaking his head. "I knew you'd last the longest. But if I can break *you*, I can break anyone."

He lifted his arm. And the pain swallowed me whole.

* * * * * * * * * * * * * * * * *

When I opened my eyes again, it was perfectly quiet and still. The darkness was absolute. Was I dead?

I was still breathing. In and out. Surely the dead had no need to breathe. I tried to stop. For a long minute, nothing happened. Then, gradually, my chest started to hurt. The pressure built and built until I had to surrender to it.

I dragged in a gulp of cool, damp air and started coughing. The back of my head exploded into life. The dull ache turned into sharp stabs between one breath and the next.

I lifted myself up onto my elbows and waited for the pain to subside a little.

"Cal? Can you hear me?"

A light was turned on. I squeezed my eyes shut against the glare, and it was moved away.

"Cal? Are you awake this time?"

This time?

"Yes," I croaked, and tried to swallow. My mouth was too dry. I felt the edge of a cup against my lips and sucked in a huge mouthful of water. I coughed again.

"That's enough," came another voice. Deeper. Albany? "Take it slowly."

I grabbed the cup with both hands and drank again. Then I felt like I was going to throw up. There was a huff of exasperation.

"I think he's awake."

Definitely Albany. I opened my eyes again and tried to adjust to the light. The rest of the unit was staring back at me.

"Hey," I said, rather foolishly.

"Do you remember what happened to you?"

I looked at Benedar. "Another nightmare, I suppose?"

A few of them exchanged glances.

"I'm sorry. I should probably sleep in the other cave."

I sat upright, reaching behind to touch the part of my head that was hurting. It was sore. My hair was all clumped together. Was that *blood*?

Well, that was embarrassing. Smashing my head open on the rock just because of a bad dream.

Benedar looked crestfallen. "You don't remember," he said in a small voice. "Which means you won't remember what happened before either."

"Before what?"

There were a few low whispers, and I began to feel nervous.

"Before *what*?"

"OK, everyone, he's obviously fine," said Albany. "Just a small memory problem. Benedar can handle it. Let's get back to sleep. We've got that big repair job tomorrow."

Grumbling, the others shuffled back to their sleeping places. Albany put his hand on Benedar's shoulder for a second and then left us alone.

"Cal…"

"Before what, Benedar?"

"Before I punched you and you hit your head on a jagged piece of rock."

My mouth fell open.

"*You* punched me?"

He nodded. I touched my head again, and suddenly realised that it wasn't a recent injury. The blood was crusted over.

"When?"

"Two nights ago."

"*Why?*"

"It was an accident. You were tickling me, and I was mad."

He shook his head. "It's what happened before that's important. Especially because of what you've been saying in your nightmares."

"Wait. I've been out cold for two days and nights?"

He nodded solemnly.

"Having nightmares the whole time?"

"It sounded like it."

"Tell me," I said.

Benedar explained what I'd written and the definition that had emerged from my mouth as if I'd been a secret Thinker all this time.

The words sounded strange. Like a different language. I stared at the word on the page, not recognising the handwriting or how to read it.

"How far back do you remember?"

I concentrated. The pain in my head kept pace with the beat of my heart, on/off like a switch.

"We were going to test if the Flyers were real. We had to wait for a day when the sun rose."

Benedar sighed. He told me what had happened. I didn't believe him. He said no one had believed *me* either.

Then he described what I'd actually said while I was unconscious. I'd used those kinds of words a lot.

"...magic shouldn't be used this way..."

"...I will fight your enchantment..."

"...I *will* be a magician again, Varun! I promise you! And you'd better start running when you see me!"

I listened with increasing shock. Benedar was reading off a long list, and I put my hand on top of the paper to stop him.

"Varun is the Breaker's name," I said.

"Albany told me," replied Benedar. "At least you remember that much."

I shook my head.

"I had no idea that my imagination was so out of control. Making up words and stories like that... I'm going to have to sleep somewhere else."

"They came out of your mouth while you were

awake first," argued Benedar. "You *linked*, Cal. I think it's real."

"No. That's impossible. My life has been lived in the childstation and the unit. The only time I've seen the Breaker up close was with Albany."

"What about Garrett?" asked Benedar.

I stiffened.

"You called for him. You tried to save him."

My expression twisted.

"In my dream, you mean," I said angrily. "I couldn't save him at his Gathering. It makes sense that I wouldn't be able to save him in my dream either."

"It didn't sound like he was your older brother in the dream."

I hunched my shoulders. "I don't want to talk about it."

Benedar looked at me for a moment and then reached behind him for a small plate of food. He handed it to me. I chewed slowly, remembering how the water had made me feel sick.

We sat in silence, until I could see that Benedar was struggling to stay awake. I set the plate on the floor, turned off the light, and lay down on my side again. He curled up next to me and fell asleep straight away.

I tested the strange words, mouthing them in the darkness. Magic. Magician. Enchant. Enchantment. Spell.

It was nonsense. Like a two-year-old when they're learning speech for the first time. I was quite sure that they weren't real.

11 The Definition Of Magic

My head got better. The nightmares gradually spaced out. I was able to shake off the tiredness that I'd been wearing like a second shirt.

I was grateful. It was bad enough that my brain created an imaginary Breaker to destroy me while I slept. But screaming out the details to the rest of the unit in the middle of the night was just humiliating.

Sometimes I remembered fragments, but they always drifted away from me in the first few seconds after waking. I couldn't hold onto them.

The age that Thinkers were summoned returned to normal. The Thinker population would be out of balance for a long time after what the Breaker had done.

The total number of Thinkers was what the Opta required it to be. One Thinker for every ten Workers. Similar to the number of Opta to Exta.

But there were too many scraps. And the

Thinkers who had died early had obviously not been replaced with Workers. We all carried an increased burden to keep the city operational.

Take my unit. We'd always been ten. Eight Workers and two Thinkers. When Benedar arrived, we'd become seven Workers and three Thinkers.

Jory and Zack. Me and Benedar. Albany and Sorvan. Dane and Maxen. Alken and Randall.

After we lost Jory and Zack, Benedar covered for them. But we never got another Worker. Seven instead of eight doesn't sound like much of a difference. We felt it though.

Benedar worked it out. Every seven days, we had to complete one extra day's work each. It was a lot. We were lucky that Benedar was so good at finding shortcuts for us.

The time came for Dane to be summoned. Albany and I didn't sleep much in the days before his Gathering, both of us wishing that we didn't know what was happening to him.

At least we could reassure Maxen. We told him that the quicker he said the four words, the less Dane would suffer. It wasn't us that killed our brothers. It was *them*. The Binder and the Breaker.

Albany became the oldest, with Alken not far behind. Those twelve years that stretched endlessly in front of us when we left the childstation were nothing really. We might as well try to hold onto rock dust. Sooner or later it trickled through our fingers, or the wind stole it from us.

Maxen came back from the childstation with a Worker. A tough little guy called Beck, who threw himself fearlessly into his first assignment as if he were ten years old, not six.

We continued to gather information. I knew that Benedar kept looking for those strange words, even though I'd told him not to. I was pretty certain that they were a side effect of touching the Flyer and then hitting my head.

I tried making up a few more, just to show him how ridiculous he was being.

"Lingle."

"Broggen."

"Yavver."

I thought it was funny. And it made me feel like I was back in control. He got quite cross, scowling at me every time I came up with a new bit of gibberish.

"Use your Thinker's brain, Benedar," I sighed. "Workers just don't know anything clever. That's the system, and it's been that way all my life. What comes out of my mouth is almost guaranteed to be rubbish."

"*No*," he said fiercely. "You might be a Worker, but you're different. I don't know why you won't put it to the test."

He wanted me to touch another Flyer. To see if it would happen again.

"I'm not putting it to the test. We should concentrate on the gaps in your charts."

I didn't want anyone to know how scared I really was underneath the joking. It was a stupid fear. Stupid just like me. I just didn't want to start saying those strange words again. I didn't want to bring the nightmares back either.

On top of the gaps in our knowledge about the city, and the Exta lifecycle, we also didn't know anything about the rest of Imbera.

We hadn't been able to confirm whether ours was the only city. We could see another shape on the horizon where the sun set.

In a world with so much water, it seemed likely that all the available land would be inhabited. But none of our contacts in the communication units had seen any messages that came from outside of our own city.

What were the chances of there being another Binder and another Breaker? Benedar said they were low. He said that our circumstances, with the Flyers and the statue and the symbols, were a very precise combination. Something that could have taken years to get right.

And because there was no regular communication with other places, it was apparently more likely that we were unique. That gave us hope.

Not much, because we had no way of travelling that far away from our little island. But maybe one day someone would be curious and come to visit us instead. It was like Garrett had told me. Hope made life bearable.

Benedar still talked about the Flyers from time to time, despite my reluctance. He asked us to start looking at the great statue on the ruling house.

He wanted some kind of proof that they had a role to play in the binding. That they were controlling us. He didn't dare use the words enchantment or spell, but I knew that's what he meant.

The others agreed. Benedar had proved his worth as a Thinker time and again. They were prepared to make allowances, even if this particular idea sounded more than a bit incredible.

We started making detours through the centre of the city whenever Benedar could fit them into our schedule. It added long minutes to our journey times, so we weren't able to do it very often.

The first time I walked past the ruling house, I had very mixed feelings. Anger, fear, helplessness. I usually only saw it at the

Gatherings. When the square was empty, it looked more like the other buildings.

Large windows, shining with Opta brilliance into the darkness. Promising warmth, good food, and a life filled with easy choices.

I imagined how the Binder spent her days when she wasn't destroying life essences. The questions she might ask herself.

What should I eat for breakfast today? What scent should I add to my bathing water? What music shall I listen to? Shall I wear the white dress, or the white dress?

All while the essences from the last Gathering were trapped below her in an underground room full of boxes. Their skills, waiting to be allocated. Her victims, and his.

I wanted to catch a glimpse of Alanna. I thought about her a lot, and what I would say to her if I saw her again. I wondered what she looked like now we were both two years older.

But I didn't dare to search for her. There was only time for a quick, cautious glance at the statue. As if I were checking the sky for signs of rain. It had to appear natural. In this part of the city, Opta eyes were everywhere.

We all looked, but none of us saw anything out of the ordinary. Until the next Gathering.

There were flames behind the statue's eyes. Every time a life essence was stolen, its eyes blazed into life. Like no light I had ever seen. I nudged Albany, who was standing next to me, and raised my eyes upwards.

He understood immediately, and the next time he saw it too. It was very fast. We could only see it if we were looking in the right place at exactly the right moment.

A flash of red fire, and then back to the flat, grey stone, as if we had imagined it. We reported it to Benedar, who nodded as if he had expected something like this.

"The Flyer obviously does more than just create the hallucinations," he said.

"What?" Albany and I said together. We exchanged a quick, embarrassed glance. Thinker words. No matter how many we tried to learn, there were always more.

The whole unit was sitting in the weak, greenish glow of our last remaining light source. It was the night before the sun rose, and our batteries had almost run out.

"Sorry," Benedar apologised. "I mean it does more than create visions."

"Why don't you just say visions then?"

Beck was frowning as he spoke. He might only have been six, but he'd asked a fair question.

"It's not quite the same. A vision is more like something you might imagine yourself. A hallucination is a malfunction. Forced on you by illness, or extreme tiredness, or maybe a sp…"

His voice trailed off as he changed his mind before he could finish the word. I gave him a disbelieving look.

"Were you actually going to say it? Spell?" I said accusingly.

I thought Benedar was blushing, but in the green light I couldn't be sure. Alken sniggered, and Albany elbowed him into silence.

"What's a spell?" said Beck.

Benedar gave me a challenging look. He obviously wanted me to answer so that he could disagree with me. I sighed.

"It's nothing," I said firmly.

"Older Brother Speak for 'I don't want to talk about it'," said Benedar, giving Beck a grin. Beck smiled back.

"Oh, you mean like 'ask me again later' or 'we'll see'? Yeah, I get that *a lot.*"

He rolled his eyes, and we all started laughing. All except Maxen, who protested loudly.

"That's not what I say to you, scrap! And even if I did, you're supposed to show me some respect."

"Let me know when you figure that one out," I said. "Three years in, and I'm still at a disadvantage."

"It's different for you," said Albany. "Benedar is a Thinker, and anyway, he belongs to all of us."

There were sounds of agreement. Benedar ducked his head, embarrassed. Sometimes I forgot how young he still was.

"What else does the statue of the Flyer do then?" I said, trying to get the conversation back on track. It was late, and tomorrow's workload would be even less forgiving if we didn't go to sleep soon.

"I think it collects life essences like a magnet."

Interesting. I'd used magnets. I knew how they worked. I'd even thought myself that life essences at Gatherings were drawn to the ruling house like metal is drawn to a magnet.

"When we see our visions of the Flyers, it's like a magnetic field that just happens to be visible.

"But it's not until the Initiation Word that the magnet grabs you. Then you are pulled towards the Binder. After that, you can't leave the statue."

We all thought about this. Zack's anguished face as he put that particular rule to the test came uninvited into my head. Benedar continued.

"Those symbols you've told me about. They must be conductors for the spell. Like the cables that take the sun's energy to the city. It all comes down to energy. Ours, theirs, the statue's."

Wait a minute. Did he say spell?

"Why does the Flyer's spell get to boss me around then?" asked Albany.

I looked at him in shock. I couldn't believe his casual acceptance of the strange word.

"It's a superior form of energy. I think it's called magic."

Benedar avoided my gaze. I was torn. Half of me was really angry at the way he was ignoring my instructions to never say those strange words again. The other half was fascinated.

"And I think the Opta are the magicians. They can control the energy called magic."

12 Random Reminders

Our chances of getting to sleep after that were non-existent. Everyone had an opinion on what magic actually was. We all knew that our only chance of ever escaping the Opta started with understanding how they kept us prisoner in the first place. The prospect of finally making some progress was exciting.

Even so, I could hardly believe how quickly the excitement took hold, and their readiness to believe in this thing called magic.

We were Workers. Our days were nothing but rock, tools, and hard labour. Yet one fantastical bedtime story and we'd suddenly become kids again.

I tried to hold back, even though their enthusiasm was contagious. I was scared. What if this turned out to be proof that we could *never* escape?

We'd come so far since Zack's Gathering. OK,

so we didn't understand how the process worked. But we could tell ourselves that once we knew, we'd be able to fight. And because of that belief, that hope, everything we did had a purpose to it.

Collecting all the information for Benedar's charts. Taking huge risks by being in the wrong place at the wrong time. Working ourselves into the ground all week to carve out a few extra moments. Making friends with a girl as if there were actually a point to it.

Take that hope away, and what did we have? Nothing. Nothing worth living for, anyway.

I kept quiet. What harm could it do to enjoy the moment? But it was very strange hearing those words spoken as part of an ordinary conversation. I'd spent weeks making sure they never stayed in my head for more than a few seconds.

The next morning, we were all utterly exhausted, starting the day as tired as we would normally end it. We were very lucky not to have any accidents during the day's assignments.

On our way back to the cave, Maxen carried Beck part of the way. He was nearly sleepwalking. We were squinting into the red glow of the sun as it slowly sank in the sky.

Our meal had been left in its usual place by the cave entrance. The food units made two deliveries a day, and we were expected to allocate it ourselves.

Dry fish? Check. A side dish that was either burnt or raw? Check. Tiny portions? Check. It was doubly insulting. Nasty food, *and* not enough of it.

Now that we had our imaginary fishing net spanning most of the city, we were sometimes able to trade information for Opta food. Benedar and Haylen helped other units to do what we were doing. Including units with access to Opta provisions.

Those were good days. If you could turn happiness into a meal, I'm pretty sure it would taste a lot like a hot meat pie.

After we'd eaten, we headed back out to the edge of the island. Tiredness or not, this couldn't wait. Everyone wanted to touch a Flyer now. To feel this magic for themselves. I had to confess that I did too.

The sun was even lower than before, turning the entire sky dark red in between the clouds. It was going to rain soon. Albany scrambled up the rocks, wanting to be first.

I stared at the ocean as the next Flyer approached me. Although I was fairly sure that they weren't real, I still tensed as it got closer, half convinced it would grab me with its huge feet and carry me off.

This one was swooping very low. I glanced at

the others, but they obviously weren't seeing what I was seeing. They were all watching Albany.

It had happened to me once before, a Flyer coming in so low that I'd ducked all the way to the ground in fear.

The Flyer was almost at shoulder level. I started cringing downwards, unable to help myself. At the last minute, I put my hands up to cover my face, and it brushed against them as it passed.

Definitely *not* a solid, scaly body. No reeking monster's breath either. More like a magnetic field.

I looked down at my hands. I wondered which one of them had touched the Flyer last time.

Benedar nudged my shoulder.

"It was the left one," he whispered with a grin.

I shook my head, reluctantly smiling back. I closed my left hand into a fist, thinking that I must be imagining the strange buzzing in my palm.

The clouds were gathering, stealing the light from the sky. There was a rumble of thunder in the distance.

"Did you plan all this?" I asked.

"Not exactly. I've been certain for a while that the Opta use a special kind of energy to make their spell work, but the pieces didn't fall into place until your report about the statue's eyes."

He huffed at my expression.

"Yes, Cal, it *is* a spell. *You* called it that."

"I called you a scrap too. Just before you punched me. Are you telling me that's true as well? *Are* you still a scrap? Huh?"

I ruffled his hair exactly how he hated it most.

He laughed, trying to twist away. Then he went still.

"You remember calling me a scrap before I punched you?"

I opened my mouth in shock, but I didn't answer him. The buzzing felt like tiny insect wings against my hand.

"How much else do you remember?" he said excitedly.

"I don't know," I replied slowly. I knew it wasn't true, even as I finished speaking. The missing memories were just suddenly *there*. All of them. Between one blink and the next.

Spell. A way to control or enchant using magic. Magic, magic, magic. Inside me and around me. The Breaker, and Garrett. The pain.

"You do remember," Benedar argued, his expression determined. "I can see that you do. It's in your eyes."

I felt a flash of annoyance. My stupid eyes again. I wanted them to be walls, and they were more like windows.

But I could hardly blame my eyes for reflecting *this*. What did it all mean? It should not be possible to have a memory of something that *did not happen to me*. Could not have happened to me.

Benedar waited.

"Yes, I remember. But it doesn't make any sense..."

I was interrupted by an enormous clap of thunder. The clouds had darkened, and heavy drops of rain started to fall. Faster and faster, until we could hardly see our hands in front of our faces.

When it rains on Imbera, it really rains. Crops that were gasping for water one day might be swimming in it the next. The only thing to do was get undercover and wait it out.

Albany slipped on his way down. The rocks were slimy with running water. He sliced open the skin near his elbow, and the rain washed the blood away in a stream of red down his arm.

By the time we got back to the cave, we were all shivering, watching the puddles forming around our feet. If it rained for long enough, they would join together like a carpet made out of freezing cold water. Our lights with their newly charged batteries were yellow and green in the gloom.

Albany tied a makeshift bandage around his arm, refusing any offers of help.

There was nothing to do but try to sleep. We were all tired anyway, and no one was going to be jumping off the rocks until the rain stopped.

Benedar looked at me enquiringly, but I shook my head.

"Tomorrow," I murmured. "We'll talk then. I need to get it straight in my head anyway."

The next day, Alken picked up our work assignment early, hoping that we could get ahead of ourselves. No chance, as it turned out.

The Opta had brought forward the cleaning rotation for the north quarter of the city. Along with some of the other building maintenance units, we'd be working flat out for days to get it done.

Lugging buckets of ocean water to and fro. Scrubbing, rinsing and then scrubbing some more. It was cold, dirty, and miserable. And grey rock is grey rock. It looks kind of dingy even when it's clean. In my opinion. Which counted for nothing, of course.

At least we got a break for an hour. Everyone had to leave the city before the glow from the Time of Assignment turned the black sky all shades of blue and green.

I looked at it with new eyes. I was certain it was another spell. I wished I could get close enough to touch the light, to see if it buzzed in the same way the Flyers did.

We ate our small ration early, and I told the others some of what I'd remembered the previous day. I tried to write the word again, and it flowed from the pen like I was a Thinker.

I hesitated for a second, then continued writing, completing the definition. The others were speechless. Albany was staring at me as if he'd never seen me before.

Benedar looked more closely at the writing and frowned.

"What?" I said self-consciously. "Did I make a mistake or something?"

"No... but your writing is weird. I mean, it's kind of old-fashioned. Like some of the manuscripts in the Book Rooms."

He pointed to the page.

"You see that curl on the A and the way the top and bottom of the letters stick out?"

He grabbed the paper and copied what I'd written in his own handwriting. I looked.

Spell. A way to enchant or control using magic.

Spell. A way to enchant or control using magic.

His handwriting was definitely better. Mine looked more like a spider had crawled across the page.

ALEX C VICK

"Write something else," suggested Alken.

But I couldn't. Outside of those words, I was as blind to reading and writing as ever. We wondered if there was some kind of magic energy attached to them. Maybe it granted an echo of Thinker intelligence.

But it didn't work on anyone else. They couldn't read it, and they couldn't write it.

"You touched the Flyer," pointed out Alken. "Maybe that's the reason you can do it."

Albany still hadn't spoken. I looked at him warily.

"It's still me," I said.

"Is it?"

"Why wouldn't it be?"

"I don't know." Albany folded his arms. "I've never heard of a Worker who can read and write."

"I *can't* read and write. One sentence doesn't make me a Thinker."

He shrugged. "I guess not." But he didn't look convinced.

I was glad I'd kept my memories of the process, and the Breaker, to myself. If Albany was looking at me suspiciously because I'd picked up a pen, he'd be *really* freaked out by the idea that I knew the Breaker personally.

Well, I was quite freaked out by the idea myself.

We returned to our cleaning. Benedar went to the Book Rooms to meet with Haylen while we worked. He was going to finally tell her about magic and the Flyers.

The rest of her unit was working nearby on the same cleaning assignment as ours. I could see Albany exchanging quick glances with Landra, the girl he liked.

Once he even managed to touch her hand for a second, as if by accident. They kept their eyes lowered, but their grins were clear for anyone to see.

Landra had yellow hair which she tied up, but curly bits were always escaping. She had small ears, and her mouth was big and smiley.

Fortunately, they got away with the hand touching. The Opta residents of the houses we were working on had yet to emerge. When they appeared at the windows, we all kept our heads down.

After the Time of Assignment, the Opta were always that bit sharper. It seemed to me like this allocation thing should make them happy. All we saw was a tendency to punish even more quickly than usual.

The Breaker and the Binder were undoubtedly in charge of our little island city. But even an ordinary Opta was still way above *us* in terms of authority.

They all knew the Initiation Word. Any one of them could say it at any time. A moment's amusement for them, and a death sentence for us.

It was surprising how different we were, considering the basics were the same. Two arms and legs, a face, hair, clothes, skin, all that stuff. Yet the differences outweighed it all.

They had old, old eyes in a young face devoid of colour and warmth. White hair, white skin, silver eyes. Strong, thanks to the stolen skills. Clever and calculating too.

I was mindlessly scrubbing the wall, half-way up a ladder that was more than slightly rickety, when I realised something. Varun hadn't always been like that.

Wait a minute, when did he become Varun? He wasn't Varun to me. *The Breaker*, I corrected hastily inside my head. The Breaker hadn't always been like that.

I tried to let the memory drift a bit, hoping that it might become clearer if I didn't concentrate on it.

The ladder wobbled, and I nearly fell. I grabbed onto the window ledge next to me, the surge of panic destroying the fragile memory completely. The Opta girl inside the room jumped slightly as I appeared at the window.

For a split second, our eyes met. I felt my

entire body go weak with shock.

"Mordra?" I whispered.

It shouldn't have been possible, but she turned even whiter.

Wait, *what* was I doing? Had I gone completely mad?

I scrabbled desperately at the ladder, trying to get away from the window. My legs and arms were shaking so much that I could hardly hold onto it.

I recognised her. I was officially losing it.

She was standing at the window now. I tensed.

"Please don't say it!" I asked frantically, and then ducked my head. You didn't address an Opta directly, and you *definitely* didn't raise your voice.

There was silence. I swallowed. Still silence. I risked a glance upwards. What I saw pushed the breath right out of my chest.

She looked guilty. She looked undecided. But more than that, she looked sad.

"Cal..." she said softly.

I was completely unnerved. I half slid, half fell down the ladder to get away. I grabbed my bucket and ran to refill it with very unsteady footsteps. My breathing didn't return to normal until I'd reached the edge of the island.

What was going on?

13 The Night Shift

All I could do was carry on. Abandoning my work assignment was not an option. Whatever miracle had allowed me to escape the Initiation Word just now was unlikely to be repeated.

There was a kind of roaring inside my head that blocked out everything else. I pushed myself to the limit, scrubbing and cleaning, not looking away from the walls of the building once.

Eventually it was time to stop. I kept my gaze on my feet the whole time we were cleaning up for the day. The walk away from the city seemed to take forever.

The conversation started up again as we got closer to what passed for home. Albany came to walk alongside me.

"What's up?"

"Nothing."

"I didn't mean to treat you like that earlier. It was just a bit crazy seeing you writing."

"I know," I said. He didn't know the half of it.

Benedar was waiting when we got back to our particular cave. He'd divided up the rest of the food into small piles and had his charts laid out in front of him.

He excitedly explained something that Haylen had told him. About a possible link between Opta age and the water.

It was decided that we had to try touching the Flyers again as soon as possible. Benedar was sure that it was the reason for my strange memory recall.

No sooner had this been agreed than we heard someone calling for us outside the cave.

"Unit one-eight-seven! Is anyone awake in there?"

Albany, as the oldest, got up to answer the summons. He returned with a boy who looked young and nervous. He was a house Exta. It was obvious from his lighter coloured clothing and clean face.

"Tell them," Albany said.

We looked at the boy curiously. I was glad of the distraction. The longer I went without talking about my strange episode at the window, the more hopeful I was that I could pretend it hadn't happened.

If I was going to start blurting out the name of every Opta I met, I would be in serious trouble. I could end up being bound before the sun even rose again.

"We need a repair done. At the ruling house. Straight away."

"What kind of repair?" said Alken.

I was hardly listening as the other boy answered. As soon as I heard "ruling house", all I could think of was Alanna. Going there for a proper reason, which didn't involve being summoned, could be my first real chance to see her again.

"...so we need at least four building Workers to come and put it back."

I stood up.

"Count me in," I said.

Albany looked at me.

"Are you sure?" he said. "I didn't think you'd want to run the risk of seeing the Breaker again."

I blushed. I was hoping the low light would hide my red face, but it seemed I wasn't that lucky.

He grinned.

"I get it. I've always wondered, and now I'm sure."

"What is it?" said Benedar, looking up at me.

"Who else is coming?" I asked, ignoring him. Just because Albany had guessed how I felt about Alanna, it didn't mean everyone else had to know.

"Me, Alken, and Sorvan," replied Albany.

"Why not me?" asked Maxen. It was a good question. He was the other older brother in the group.

"Because someone has to stay behind and make sure this lot doesn't get into trouble. Anyway, Sorvan's not that much younger than you."

This was true. Albany was a long way past his seventeenth birthday already. Which made Sorvan not far behind Maxen.

We walked through the quiet city, following the boy back to the ruling house.

"Why did they send you?" I said. "You don't work there."

He glanced back at me.

"My master is one of the Opta elders who also lives in the square. And how would you know if I work at the ruling house or not?"

"I know Alanna," I said before I could help myself.

He looked at me a bit more closely.

"Really?"

I nodded awkwardly. "Sort of. Well, not really. Um, hardly at all I suppose…"

Albany stifled a laugh. The boy's expression showed that he thought I was an idiot, but was too polite to say so.

When we got there, we stopped and stared.

The main door had been ripped off its hinges. It was like some kind of giant with incredible strength had pushed it aside. Solid stone, as thick and heavy as the walls, just moved out of the way.

I wasn't sure that four of us would be enough to move it back. Even with our tools. Albany sent Sorvan to fetch the trolley and levers. We weren't going to be able to lift it ourselves.

"How did it happen?" I asked.

Before the boy could open his mouth, a silhouette appeared in the doorway. I felt a shiver on the back of my neck. It was *him*.

"You are finished here, Nadin, are you not?"

The boy didn't hesitate. He darted into the house next door as quickly as if there were someone chasing him.

The Breaker looked at us. Seeing him in person brought the memories crashing back. Two or three seconds at a time, exploding in my head one after the other.

"Varun," I whispered, feeling sick to my stomach.

He stepped into the light.

"Cal. How nice to see you again. And your friend too. This *is* a day of surprises."

His words were ordinary. Pleasant even. But the expression on his face was the same as when he scooped out a life essence. Evil anticipation.

Twisted excitement.

Fortunately it killed my flashbacks like a bucket of ocean water dumped on my head. I tumbled back into the real me and shut my mouth immediately.

"The fact that it should be *your* unit chosen by Nadin for this repair... I wonder if it really is coincidence? Or is it more like fate?"

We looked at him blankly, not knowing what he was talking about. My heart was still racing.

"Do you know what fate is, Cal?"

I nodded carefully. I knew that my fate was to be bound. We were told at the childstation that we could not escape our fate.

He gave me a nasty smile.

"No, I am not asking if you know what *your* fate is. You would have to be an idiot even by Exta standards not to know that. I want to know if you understand the *idea* of fate."

We all remained silent, figuring that it was the safer option. He could insult us as much as he wanted, if it meant that we would be allowed to leave when he was done.

"I thought not. The idea of fate is possibly a little beyond what the breeding programme has allowed you to retain."

What was he talking about now? How could the breeding programme allow me to *keep* anything? No one existed before they were born.

"However, the fact that your skills and theirs should be within my grasp at almost the same moment... I will have to consider this further."

There was a horrified intake of breath from Albany. Was he threatening to bind us right now?

The Breaker merely smirked.

"Albany, isn't it? I am not talking about you. You are already in your eighteenth year in any case. I will take your life soon enough. I mean *you*."

He stared at me. As our eyes met, I felt the panic rise. I tried to look away, but it was like his gaze had bound me already. I was scared that my eyes were telling him everything. Maybe he could see what we had discovered about spells and magic.

"There are two Exta newly bound to the ruling house this evening. You can see the evidence of their physical strength before you."

He gestured to the ruined door, breaking eye contact, and I wanted to gasp with relief. Albany and Alken exchanged glances, with identical expressions of doubt. Two Exta could not have moved this door on their own.

"You will return the door to its rightful place, and then you will leave. You will not think about my new guests. You will not look for them, and you will most certainly not talk to them.

"If I learn that you have disobeyed me, I will

see it as evidence that Cal's skills and theirs are complementary. I will have no hesitation in binding him too."

He left without giving us another glance, completely confident that we would carry out his orders, and with good reason. My curiosity about the two Exta could hardly compete with the fear of being bound myself.

Quite apart from the fact that this was my life he was talking about, our unit was already down to seven Workers. We could not lose another.

Sorvan returned with the trolley, and we set about our work. It was hard going. There was no sound coming from either inside the house or the square outside.

Once the fear of the Breaker subsided, it was replaced with a hollow feeling of disappointment in my stomach. It didn't look like I was going to be able to see Alanna.

Suddenly someone appeared from inside the house. It was a boy about the same age as me. He marched up to us with an energy and authority that I had never seen before.

We all tried not to look at him, the Breaker's warning still ringing in our ears, but he was quite insistent. Question after question. He sounded like a Thinker. I tried to push him away without speaking, but he didn't move.

Eventually I turned to look, and I stiffened in

shock. He was dressed from head to toe in black, and I could almost see his life essence radiating off him. Even his green eyes glittered slightly.

He lifted one hand impatiently to his black hair and pushed it off his forehead. His expression was completely fearless.

"Can you help us understand what is happening here? If you could only—"

I interrupted him desperately.

"We cannot help you! There is no ending the spell once you have been bound. We would only be hastening our own donations. And my unit cannot do without me yet. My brother is too young."

I didn't know why I was explaining. I suppose I felt sorry for him. He obviously didn't understand the seriousness of his situation. I hesitated.

Where had he come from if he didn't know what was happening to him? Another city? Was this finally the proof that our small island wasn't alone in the ocean?

"The outcome is the same whether you fight or not. So don't," I said.

"Of course I'm going to fight! There must be a way to resist this."

His green eyes were wide. He was so confident. But it was surely only ignorance that allowed him to be this determined.

"Everyone thinks that until the pain starts. I've seen bigger and braver than you change their minds in a split second."

He blinked. He knew what I meant about the pain then.

I turned to carry on with my work, seeing Albany's furious gaze out of the corner of my eye. I had already spent far too long talking.

"Wait!" said the boy. "What did you say about your own donations? Is this going to happen to you too?"

His voice was urgent and honest. It was hard to believe, but it seemed that he really did not know. There was a symbol on the shoulder of his shirt. It was a seven-pointed star, apparently glittering with the same energy as his life force.

I was starting to wish that I could talk to him properly. He was different. Not an Exta like us. Not an Opta either.

I suddenly realised that he had accepted my earlier use of the word "spell" without comment. He might know about this thing called magic. He might... but no. It wasn't worth dying for.

"It happens to all Exta," I explained hastily. "They take our life essences early, when we are physically strong.

"If you are selected for breeding, or if you have a non-physical talent that requires development, then you might live to twenty. But

I don't expect that to happen to me."

Albany was glaring at me now, still not quite daring to look straight at the boy, but bristling with suppressed anger.

I didn't know why I was telling the boy so much. Yes, I felt sorry for him, but it wasn't as if I owed him an explanation. It wasn't my fault he was here.

He was looking back at me as if he was starting to understand. He was lost for words.

"Don't ask me anything else, because I won't answer," I said fiercely.

"If we're not done before they get back, he might say the Initiation Word to punish us, and then I'll be bound just like you. I'm sorry, stranger."

I turned my back again, and this time the boy walked away with slow footsteps. I heard a girl's voice raised in question. I gritted my teeth, resisting the temptation to turn round and see what she looked like.

I wondered if she was wearing her force field like it was a layer of clothing as well. Did she have a strange symbol on her shoulder? Did she know all about magic?

My head was still buzzing with questions when we finished our work. We tested the door a few times, to double-check that it was completely repaired.

Just as we were about to leave the square, Nadin reappeared. We looked at him warily. What now?

He pointed at me.

"Alanna wants to talk to you."

14 The More I Learn The Less I Know

I tried to keep my face still, but my heart was suddenly crashing around in my chest again. I'd spent two years thinking about Alanna, and now in a few moments I was finally going to see her again. I swallowed nervously.

Maybe if I swallowed enough times, I'd be able to stop myself from saying anything really stupid.

"Just you though," continued Nadin. "It's too dangerous if all of you stay."

Albany frowned.

"There is something going on with you lately, Cal. The writing, the weird new words, the nightmares... just be careful."

I nodded. Although being careful and hanging around the ruling house to have a forbidden conversation probably didn't go very well together.

The other three walked away, and I followed Nadin to the entranceway of his house. He was shorter and thinner than me, and he darted ahead so quickly that I struggled to keep up.

We descended underground, through a small door off the main hallway. I wanted to ask where we were going, but didn't dare to make any noise.

The room we ended up in looked very similar to Alanna and Kaylar's, and I realised that this must be where Nadin lived. There was a smaller boy asleep in the corner. Nadin continued walking into the shadows, and I saw an archway.

They were connected. All the Exta rooms beneath the houses in the central square. I hadn't noticed the archways before.

Nadin indicated that I should walk through.

I could feel my forehead prickling with nervous sweat. I wondered if I were covered in rock dust from repairing the door. I really wished I were someone else. Someone who knew what to say and how to behave.

Nadin looked at me impatiently.

I walked through.

"Er… hi," I said. *Stop staring, Cal. Stop staring.*

I was grinning like an idiot. I tried not to, but my whole face felt numb. Like it didn't belong to me.

She was standing still. Almost as tall as me

now. Her shiny brown hair was longer and tied up with black-and-white ribbons. Her eyes were amazing. I could *not* stop staring at her.

"They have no identifier," she said.

I opened my mouth, but no words came out.

"Do you understand what that means?" she continued.

"Um. Well. Um. I suppose…"

What was wrong with me?

"What's wrong with you?" she asked.

"That's funny, because I was just asking myself the same question…"

I trailed off at the eye roll she gave me.

"We don't have long. I have to prepare their quarters for sleeping. Kaylar's waiting for me."

She paused, checking that I was paying attention.

"The boy and girl upstairs. Newly bound. But no identifier."

She pulled up her sleeve and pointed to where the ten-digit code was hidden. Without the special light, we couldn't see it.

"There are no Exta in this city without an identifier. They're added at birth. Haven't you found that out yet? With your network of informers?"

"You know about that?"

She gave a small smile.

"Yeah. I think it's pretty impressive actually.

We've been working on something similar, in the square, but we don't have the same reach as you. Or as many Thinkers."

My mouth was open again. I tried to close it.

"Cal," she said. "No time, remember?"

Her smile was definitely getting a bit bigger.

"Right," I said, smiling back. "So... no identifier. They're from somewhere else? Another city?"

"Or another world."

"*What?*"

"They arrived during the Time of Assignment. We heard them move the door. But *they* didn't move it. It was some kind of silver energy cloud. Nadin saw it."

He nodded.

"Like sparkling fog."

I tried to picture it.

"A spell?" I suggested.

She frowned.

"What's a spell?"

Finally a question I knew how to answer.

"A way to control or enchant using magic."

She looked at me for a moment. Then she shook her head in frustration.

"You'll have to wait for me. We have no time to talk about this now, and I want to know *everything.*"

I could sense Nadin's disagreement even

before he spoke.

"Alanna…"

She turned to him.

"The Breaker hasn't come down here for months. You know he hasn't."

"And my master? He checks all the time. Every room. No mixing between boys and girls, remember?"

Alanna stared at me.

"It's up to you. How brave are you feeling?"

Was she serious? This new Alanna was making my head spin.

"As brave as you," I said forcefully.

"Really? We'll see. Wait with Nadin, and I'll be back as soon as I can."

She stepped past me, and I stared after her until she disappeared from sight.

Then I realised that Nadin was smirking.

"What?" I said.

"You like her."

"No I don't," I lied.

We waited in silence for a few minutes.

"What's with the black-and-white outfits?" I said eventually.

Nadin was wearing the same colour combination as Alanna.

"White to please the eyes of our masters. Black to remind ourselves that we are Exta and belong in the dirt."

He recited it as if he had heard it many times before.

I raised my eyebrows.

"Nice," I said sarcastically.

"Yeah, it gets kind of boring after a while."

His face looked a bit more friendly than before, so I carried on talking.

"Tell me what you saw. When they moved the door, I mean."

"I only looked when I heard the noise. The silver stuff was coming from one of the girl's hands. The boy was holding her other hand. Like they were doing it together."

They were magicians, then. Like the Breaker. Able to manipulate magic. I wished I had seen it for myself.

"How do you know about the identifier?" I asked.

"Alanna heard them talking about it after the Breaker had gone. She'd been told to stay away. But I guess you can see that she doesn't always do what she's told."

"She used to," I said.

Nadin obviously didn't believe me.

"How long have you known her?" I said.

"I've only been an older brother for a year. I didn't know her properly before then."

"I met her two years ago. Trust me, she was following the rules then."

"She's the leader," said Nadin. "Of our information collecting, I mean. She takes the most risks, and she has the best ideas."

"She is kind of amazing," I replied.

"Who is?"

I spun round and blushed all the way up to my eyebrows. Alanna was standing right there. I'd forgotten that her indoor shoes made no noise.

"Who is?" she repeated. Was I imagining it, or did she look a bit annoyed?

Nadin laughed.

"You are," he said.

OK, now she was blushing too. Was that a good thing? Did it mean she was angry with me? Or did it mean she might, possibly, maybe, like me too?

She raised her chin. She glared at me, like she was daring me to ask. I lost my nerve and said nothing.

Kaylar appeared behind her. She was yawning her head off, and Alanna gave her a gentle push in the direction of one of the blankets.

Then she turned back to me.

"What is magic?" she asked.

I told her what I knew. The Flyers, Benedar's theory, and the writing. I hesitated, and then mentioned my nightmares about the Breaker.

I saw her and Nadin recoil slightly when I said I thought I knew him somehow. I decided not to mention Mordra.

We all agreed that the Flyers could be made of the same energy that had ripped the great door off its hinges.

Alanna had wanted to listen to the otherworlders for longer, but she'd been afraid of hearing the Initiation Word.

She said that the boy and girl had still been awake when she had passed their room just now. She'd heard voices and seen more flashes of silver around the edges of the door. It must have been coming from them. They were definitely magicians.

The Exta were not. That much was clear. It was never going to be a fair fight for us against the Opta. But how could other magicians be bound so easily?

"What if they break just as easily?" I said. "What if the Opta get *their* skills at the next Gathering?"

Suddenly Nadin gasped and gestured urgently to Alanna. I looked at him in confusion as he backed away. I didn't hear anyone coming. She reacted immediately, shoving me towards the blankets.

"Get down," she hissed. I started to kneel, not sure exactly what I should be doing.

"Down!" she repeated, pushing my shoulders until I was on the floor. She covered me with a blanket and then leaned against me.

For a few seconds, there was no sound. I could feel the warmth of her back through the blanket. Then there was a voice.

"Still awake?"

I froze. Something about that voice was really familiar. But how could it be?

"Yes, Opta leader."

Alanna's voice was timid. Nothing like the assertive tone she'd used earlier.

"Does the Breaker know that you keep such late hours?"

His name appeared in my head. Groven. Like with Mordra, I couldn't say how or why I knew it, I just did.

And the realisation came with a creeping fear. Either I was going mad, or there was some link between me and the Opta. I wasn't sure which option was preferable.

"I will go to sleep immediately, Opta leader. I am sorry for being awake so late."

"Hmmm. See that you do. After all, there is hardly any point to your being conscious when the ruling house does not require your attention."

I felt her back go rigid. She didn't appreciate being spoken to like that. I could hardly blame her.

"Yes, Opta leader."

Her voice remained the same, but I could feel

a tug on the blanket as it was scrunched up in her fist.

Then there was silence. It went on for a long time before she finally stood up and uncovered me. We were alone again.

"Sorry," she said abruptly, obviously furious. "I can't let them see…"

"I get it," I said reassuringly. "If they saw how much you'd changed, they'd bind you. And it doesn't matter how much we've learned. Unless we figure out how to stop the binding, we're as powerless as we ever were."

Nadin reappeared.

"He has to leave," he said. "Right now."

"But I haven't even told him…"

"It doesn't matter, Alanna," said Nadin, at the same time as I said "Told me what?"

"Your box isn't empty," she said.

"*What?*"

I flashed back to the underground room and the rows of white boxes with their rainbow-coloured life essences inside.

"It has to be empty. I'm here," I said stupidly.

"I know. But the box is holding something. There's a second container in all of them."

"He has to leave. Before my master comes back."

Nadin spoke even more forcefully than before.

"Typical Groven," I said, frustrated. "He

always had a talent for sticking his big nose where it wasn't supposed to go."

They both stared at me, eyes wide. I swallowed. But it was too late to push down the words. They'd appeared in my head from nowhere, and like an idiot I had blurted them out loud.

"How do you know what the Opta call him?" said Alanna. "*How?*"

"I don't know," I said helplessly. "I just do. Like I know I've met the Breaker before. When Varun was his only name."

Alanna closed her eyes for a moment. She opened them again with a determined expression.

"You'll have to come back. Every night, until we've figured this out."

She looked at me.

"Can you handle that? It will be a big risk. You can't build walls inside your head like I can."

Nadin was shaking his head at the same time as I was nodding mine. I was trying to stop myself from grinning.

Seeing Alanna every day would be worth any kind of risk. For a few seconds, I forgot all about the boxes and my weird memory recall.

We said goodbye very quickly. I stared at her mouth, wondering what it would feel like if I kissed it.

When I lifted my gaze to her eyes again, I

could see the laughter in them.

"Maybe next time," she said.

15 The Otherworlders

But the following day was nothing like I expected. It was only half-way through the morning when Nadin came back to get us. Apparently the Breaker had been quite specific. It had to be me and Albany. And we had to come to the ruling house immediately.

I asked the others to let Benedar know. When they returned to the cave for the half-day meal, he'd be waiting, desperate for more details about what I'd learned the night before.

He'd been fast asleep when I got back, and there'd hardly been time to tell him anything when we all woke up. When he heard about the second container in the boxes, he'd been full of questions.

The others had been more interested in the magic energy, wishing that they could go to the edge of the island and touch a Flyer right then and there. The prospect of spending the day scrubbing and cleaning instead had disappointed everyone.

Albany and I followed Nadin back to the centre of the city. I was really nervous. Had the Breaker found out about my meeting with Alanna the night before? Had I dragged Albany into something that wasn't his fault?

When we arrived, Nadin directed us to a room we knew only too well. We had spent a long time watching the Breaker torture Zack and the other Thinkers behind that door.

With an apologetic look, Nadin left straight away. The Breaker acted pleased to see us, and that made me even more nervous. He beckoned us into the room. When he opened his mouth, I flinched, certain he was going to say the Initiation Word.

Then I noticed the boy from yesterday. He was *glaring* at the Breaker. I was shocked. His spirit, when he must know it was pointless, was quite remarkable.

There was a girl with him. She had long brown hair, large brown eyes, and a very downcast expression. She was wearing a purple top with white writing on it and brightly coloured shoes with thick purple string laced across them.

She had no star on her clothes. But then I noticed some silver stars in her ears that were just like the one on the boy's shirt. Maybe it was some kind of bond between them.

I saw all of this in quick sideways glances, too scared to look directly at them in case it angered the Breaker. He only had to say the Initiation Word, and I'd be joining them.

"Just in case, hmmm?" the Breaker said, his voice smooth.

"Any attempt you make to escape, and I will bind them with you. Then you'll carry the weight of their life essences on your conscience."

I froze in shock, staring at the floor. My life was now in the hands of these strangers? Albany's too? What if they tried to run away?

Albany was sent to fetch two buckets of ocean water.

"In case you pass out on me," the Breaker said to the otherworlders. He was lit up with anticipation. Much more than I'd ever seen him before, and that was saying something.

After that, it was the same living nightmare. Torture. Pain. Albany and I, side by side, forced to look. Trying to let our eyes slide out of focus so we couldn't see their faces. If I'd been in any doubt that the boy and girl were bound, I wasn't anymore.

They were brave, though. It took the Breaker ages to get the boy to make any kind of sound. But once he'd managed it, there was no stopping him. His thin white fingers repeated the same pressure and pattern against his symbols over and over.

The girl was going to faint. I could see her body relaxing. The Breaker turned to me and pointed impatiently to the ocean water. Keeping my face expressionless was almost impossible.

There was a second when I considered not doing it, but one raised white eyebrow from the Breaker and I gave in. I closed my eyes and threw the water over her, wincing when she screamed.

After that, the Breaker had them. She promised to give him whatever he wanted. The boy said nothing, obviously putting all his efforts into remaining silent.

When the Breaker lifted his hand away from his symbols, there was silence. My jaw started to ache, as I'd been clenching it all this time.

The boy grabbed the girl's hand, apparently trying to comfort her, and the Breaker laughed. Then he offered them the Binder's symbols if they answered his questions. I could see from their faces just how much they wanted it.

At that final piece of evidence, I felt a wave of frustration wash over me. It appeared that there was no chance of the otherworlders fighting the process. I made my hands into fists.

The boy looked at me then. His expression was desperate. His green eyes were glittering again, scared and angry at the same time. I stared back at him for a second and then looked down at the floor.

The Breaker was talking.

"Whatever your impressive skills, and wherever you come from, you'll be pleading for the Gathering just like the rest soon enough."

So the Breaker didn't know where they came from either. Interesting. Then, before the Breaker could ask any questions, the boy said something extraordinary.

"We *are* magicians, and we *do* come from another world."

I stared at him in utter amazement, and so did Albany. The boy sounded like he was answering a question that the Breaker had already asked. But he was also answering *our* questions. According to this boy, magicians and other worlds were real.

"An excellent start. And where do you come from *exactly*?"

The Breaker looked delighted.

"That doesn't matter," said the boy. "We can show you how to do the spells we know. There aren't many of them, after all."

Spells! I wanted to run back to Benedar and tell him.

"But we came here by mistake," the boy continued. "Even if we hadn't got drawn in by the dragons, we would still be stuck here. There's no way back to where we came from."

Dragons? What were dragons? And how did you travel to another world by *mistake*?

Apparently the Breaker found this part hard to believe as well.

"Do not lie to me," he said. "Do you think I cannot tell the difference? I have tortured thousands of Exta. I know what the truth sounds like."

I clenched my jaw again. Thousands, he said. Like it was nothing. And that was a number bigger than any I could imagine. Benedar had told me that you had to add ten to ten to ten, over and over, all day long, to get anywhere near a thousand.

The girl was trying to talk through the pain as the Breaker traced his symbols again. Something about spellstations and portals, and not being able to open them herself.

I couldn't really follow it. Was a spellstation full of spells like the childstation was full of children? And what was a portal? She said you opened it. Some kind of door then. But a door to where? Another world?

I took a deep breath as I considered the possibilities. Imagine if we could escape the Breaker just by opening a door to a place where he couldn't go. A door that could go anywhere.

Now the Breaker was asking them who the better magician was. I saw them hesitate, trying to decide how to answer. I could have told them that it was impossible to fight this. That as soon as the Binder's symbols hit them again, they would be in a trance. They'd tell him whatever he asked.

The boy claimed to be the better magician, arguing that the Breaker didn't need the girl. She disagreed, which gave the Breaker another chance to laugh at their loyalty to each other.

Then he changed the subject.

"How did you move the door yesterday?" he asked.

"With a Movement Spell," the girl answered.

"I see. And which of you did the spell?"

The girl admitted that it had been both of them. Nadin had told me as much the night before.

The Breaker's pale eyes gleamed.

"It did take both of you then? Interesting. And yet you say that you are the better magician?" he said to the boy. "I don't quite understand. I think you'll have to demonstrate it for me."

The boy and girl exchanged anxious looks. There was obviously more to this than I realised. The Breaker turned to the Binder, and she stepped forward.

Then the Breaker said something that I could hardly believe. He said that this would be the fourth time the boy and girl would receive the

Binder's symbols in less than a day.

That was too many too quickly. It was supposed to be once after being bound. Once that evening. But not again until the second evening.

What was going to happen to them? Would this break them? The Breaker wouldn't be able to question them if they were broken.

It didn't take long. They held onto each other, collapsing onto the floor. Just the way I'd seen it before. The boy tried to stand up, and could not. The Breaker made fun of them, and my heart sank.

Then he turned to me and Albany and told us to leave.

"Go. We no longer need your presence, and you have seen and heard enough. Report back to your unit. The next Gathering will yield skills the likes of which this world has never seen."

I looked at the boy, who managed to raise his head. I wished I could help him. I felt a strange mixture of admiration and pity.

We left the room, and the door closed behind us. I started to descend the staircase on shaky legs, my thoughts all over the place. Albany was already half-way out of the front door when I heard Alanna's voice.

"Cal!" she whispered urgently.

My heart leapt to see her again so

unexpectedly. Albany gave me a frustrated look.

"We can't stay," he said quickly. "We'd be mad to hang around after that little scene upstairs."

"What's happening?" Alanna asked, keeping her voice low.

I tried to explain as quickly as I could. Her eyes lit up when I told her that the strangers did come from another world. Albany shuffled his feet impatiently.

When I said that the Breaker had just started his proper questioning, Alanna suddenly took hold of my arm. I started in surprise at the feel of her hand. Her fingers were cool and smooth. She instantly lifted her hand away, and I wanted to grab hold of it and put it back.

"You can listen," she said excitedly. "The room next door, they don't use it very often. It has an air vent, and you'll be able to hear their voices."

"No," said Albany immediately. "No way."

I looked between the two of them.

"You go back," I said to Albany, and he sighed.

"What do I tell Benedar if the Breaker finds you?"

"He won't," I said. "I'll be careful."

"Yeah, that's what you promised last night. I think your idea of careful is a bit different from mine."

He shook his head, then left.

Two minutes later Alanna had shown me to the room. It was in complete darkness, and the air smelt old, like no one had breathed it for a long time. We had agreed that she wouldn't stay. The Breaker could call on her at any time, whereas I probably wouldn't be missed for a while yet.

I listened to the Breaker's relentless questions, curled up in a corner of the room, trying to breathe as quietly as possible. His voice came through the small holes in the wall quite clearly.

The boy and girl were answering him in blank, expressionless voices. Not quite broken yet. The boy said Shannon a lot. That had to be the girl's name. They called their world Androva. They were talking about things that even my wildest imaginings could not have created.

Spells that could manipulate the surrounding world and everyone in it. Spells that could be drunk, spells that changed colour, spells that could be touched. Spells that could freeze a person where they stood.

Portals to anywhere. Doorways of magical energy that connected worlds. Even a Communication Spell that allowed the force field to be shared with another person.

My head was spinning so much with all these incredible details that at first I didn't realise what was happening. The girl was resisting. She had stopped answering.

That shouldn't have been possible. It took a very long time for anyone to come out of their trance. If they ever did, of course. Some people stayed that way until they broke. And yet she was silent.

Finally the Breaker ran out of questions. He and the Binder started to make plans to take other cities, confirming our suspicions that ours was not the only island on Imbera.

Then the Binder suggested that they take the otherworlders' home as well. I put my hand over my mouth in shock. Two seconds later, I was very glad that I did, because the girl started arguing.

There was a small noise of disbelief forming in the back of my throat, and I pressed my hand more closely against my mouth. She was *arguing* with him.

OK, she wasn't arguing like a Thinker or anything, but her mental strength was still astonishing.

The Breaker knew it too. He was comparing her to the boy.

"He is nowhere near as recovered as you are. You are something of a surprise, actually."

Just a bit. She was the first person to resist the process that I had ever heard of.

Then he told her he would carry on until she gave in. He laughed at her, promising to return once she'd had all night to worry about it.

All of a sudden, they were leaving the room, and I shrank back into my corner. My excitement at hearing someone finally stand up to the Breaker vanished. If they found me, they would bind me.

I didn't hear them go down the stairs. There was only silence. The longer it went on, the more scared I got. What if they knew I was in here and were standing outside waiting for me to come out?

Time passed. My legs started to ache, and I had to straighten them. My breathing seemed to get louder and louder, and I forced myself to calm down.

I could tell from the sounds outside that the day was coming to an end. I was going to have to move. If I didn't return to my unit, my absence would be noticed.

I got to my feet, trying to remain silent. My left boot squeaked as I put my weight on it. At that moment, the door started opening in front of me, and I was so scared that I jumped back against the wall behind me with a thud.

I was incredibly relieved to see that it was Alanna. She held her finger to her lips, and I nodded to show that I understood. She walked up to me and whispered in my ear. Her breath tickled.

"They've called a meeting of the fifteen Opta elders. They've both left already. Go next door. See if you can help."

I pulled back. "If they've left, then why are you whispering?"

She glared at me.

"Because *I've* been told not to go near the otherworlders. But they've already seen you. If they mention you during questioning, it won't give you away. If they mention *me*, on the other hand…"

I made a face, understanding.

"Sorry."

She gave me an exasperated look. But after a few seconds, her expression changed, and I held my breath. Her eyes gleamed in the low light coming from the doorway.

Then she kissed me.

16 Shannon

I pushed the door open. The girl was sitting quietly, watching the boy. He was obviously still in the trance. She looked incredibly sad.

"Excuse me?" I said softly, and she jumped. At first she looked at me with fear in her eyes, and then she recognised me.

She stood up, and I pushed my hair off my forehead. It was a completely wasted gesture, because my black curls would just spring straight back, but I didn't really know what I was doing.

My head was still shouting "She kissed me!"

It was like the buzz from touching a Flyer. It felt like sunshine was trapped inside my chest. With an effort, I dragged my mind back to the girl.

"I know you, don't I?" she said. "You were there before. You threw the water over us."

I frowned. The guilt washed away all remaining thoughts of my first kiss. I apologised

177

and tried to explain why I had to follow orders. How important it was that my brother got the chance to keep linking for as long as possible.

She nodded.

"Jax told me. I know you're a prisoner as much as we are. Why did you come back? What do you want?"

She was raising her voice.

"Surely it's obvious I can't even help myself, let alone you," she continued.

I looked behind me at the door, worried that someone would hear her.

"I... I told your friend... Jax, you said? Is that his name?"

It was a strong name. It suited him.

"I told him not to fight it. But I changed my mind."

"What do you mean?" she asked.

"I thought you were Exta from a different city. I didn't know you were from another world. So I hid myself after the Opta leader sent us away. And then I heard you resist the questioning."

She scowled at me and denied it.

"I told that creepy Varun guy everything!" she complained.

"No," I said. "It might have felt that way, but you did not. You stopped talking. That alone demonstrates unimaginable power. Then you tried to argue with him."

She shook her head again.

"I said a couple of sentences."

"You don't understand," I said, frustrated that I couldn't explain it properly. "Most are like Jax. They take one full day and night before they return to themselves.

"He, the leader, knows this. And he also knows you are different. He thinks it will be fun to break you. So you have to fight back before he does."

She thought for a moment, frowning. Her eyebrows were very sharply defined, as if someone had drawn them with a pen.

Then she drew in a breath and looked at me.

"Wait... one full day and night? Before Jax comes back?"

I nodded.

"Your process was fast. Four times with her symbols, and once with his. You shouldn't even be capable of talking to me now."

She told me that it made no sense. That the boy was by far the better magician. I shrugged, not able to explain it any more than she could.

"I do have a strong force field," she said, "but I would have thought that just makes me more likely to be overpowered."

Then she did the most amazing thing I'd ever seen in my life. She held out her hands, and they filled with a glittering silver energy cloud. It expanded into the space between us.

It swirled in the air as if it were alive. Carefully, I reached out a hand to touch it. Gaining in confidence, I moved my hand back and forth, feeling it tingling against my palm.

Briefly I closed my eyes as a memory appeared inside my head with some force.

"Cal," said a woman. She had kind eyes. Something gold in her hair. She was older than anyone I'd ever seen before. There were small lines on her face.

"You're a magician now," she said. "You've been accepted at the Academy. Your father and I are very proud of you."

I had to steel myself against a wave of emotion. Grief. Regret. Tinged with a sense of wonder at seeing her face again. Because I knew her. I had known her...

Then it was gone.

Before I had time to figure out what had just happened, the girl was speaking again.

"How do you suggest I fight it then...? What's your name?"

She looked at me expectantly and I tried to concentrate.

"My name is Callax, but my friends call me Cal. And I know you are Shannon. He, Jax, he used your name many times in his answers.

"You did not use his. Another example of how

you were more in control than you realised."

"It's of no use to me if I don't know how I did it," she said, her anger returning.

I told her they should both have some food, remembering what Alanna had said when I was here before. Everyone forgets to eat and drink, she'd said, and it only makes them weaker.

We descended the stairs to the room below, Jax following us slowly. I was desperate to hold onto the strange memory, but it seemed to be slipping away from me.

Father, she'd said. I'd never heard the word before, but somehow I knew that *father* was a man. Older than a boy. Older than me. And she was… I couldn't remember the word. But I knew that she was important.

Shannon was asking me questions, in between mouthfuls of food and water. Jax ate what she put in front of him, silent and obedient.

I told her about Imbera, and the Gathering, and how we Exta lived our lives until we were bound. About the constant darkness, and the red sun. She asked me about magic and my own force field. I was confused.

"My force field is my life essence," I said.

"*My* force field is my magic," she said in return.

"I am not a magician," I replied.

"But the spell, the enchantment binds you just

the same. Varun said it attached to our force fields. You must have *some* form of magic inside you."

"No. Magic is not a word I even knew until very recently. It cannot be so."

She was silent for a moment.

"Why don't the other Opta get bound by the enchantment when the… what did you call it? When the Initiation Word is spoken?"

I admitted that I didn't know. Probably because they were more clever than us. They had all the power.

Shannon was unimpressed. Despite everything I had told her, the spark of defiance had returned to her eyes. She called me brave, and it made me embarrassed. I doubted that I would be as brave as her when my time came to be bound.

She told me that the Binder's symbols were very hard to resist. She shifted uncomfortably as she said it, and I remembered Zack's description. How he had said he would do anything if they were offered to him again.

I tried to encourage her. She could only try. And I would tell Benedar that other worlds did exist. Perhaps others would come. Perhaps we could contact them somehow.

Suddenly I heard Alanna's voice from behind the doorway.

"Cal!" she said urgently. "Cal, he's coming!"

I wasted no time. After a hasty "Good luck!" to Shannon, I ran. Alanna pulled me after her, behind the door that led to her underground room.

Only seconds later, we heard the sound of the heavy front door opening and closing. The key scraped in the lock slowly, and I panicked for a moment, before remembering I could escape through Nadin's house as I'd done before.

Across the narrow strip of light around the edges of the door, we saw the shadows of the Binder and the Breaker pass by. His self-important voice carried easily to where we were standing.

He was surprised that they had been eating and drinking. I held my breath, wondering if he would suspect that they had had help. Alanna was still holding my hand, and she squeezed it as if she knew what I was thinking.

But the Breaker quickly moved on to talk about the meeting of Opta elders that he had just attended. I listened anxiously as he described their intentions.

They were going to open a portal, that very evening. Or rather, they were going to get Jax and Shannon to do it. Androva, where the otherworlders had come from, would be joined to Imbera by a magical doorway.

At first I was excited, thinking that surely the

Breaker could not fight a world full of magicians? It could be our chance of escaping!

But then I realised that he was going to open the portal under the ocean. It would flood Androva with cold salt water, drowning any chance its inhabitants would have to resist.

My heart sank. Shannon tried to argue, her horrified voice rising. Alanna pulled at my arm.

"What?" I whispered, frowning because I didn't want to miss what the Breaker was saying.

"He's going to use *these* stairs," she whispered back. "This is the way to all the underground rooms, not just mine. We have to move!"

She started climbing down, and I followed her, half stumbling because I didn't know the dark staircase as well as she did.

We heard the door opening above us. As I glanced back, I saw the beam of yellow from the Breaker's hand held light. I descended the last few stairs as silently as I could, wincing as my feet scraped against the stone. My Worker's boots were not designed to be quiet.

We ducked into Alanna's room, and she covered me with the same blanket as before. Kaylar sleepily asked Alanna what was happening.

Alanna urged her to be still, and we all waited, expecting that any moment the Breaker would appear, the Initiation Word on his lips.

I tried to recall the strange memory. There was a name in my head for the older female, hovering just out of reach.

Father and…

Father and…

Mother? Was that what she was called? I repeated it silently. My lips formed the strange word hesitantly at first and then with increased confidence.

But who were they? And how did they know me? My chest ached. I felt a sense of loss that I couldn't explain. My head started to ache as well, as if the fragments of memory were like Worker boots, kicking against it.

Eventually I thought enough time had passed. I threw off the blanket, and Kaylar gave a squeak of surprise.

"I should go," I said reluctantly, knowing that it would be stupid to push my luck any further.

Alanna looked as angry as I felt. Wanting to fight, but powerless against the threat of the process. It was getting to the point that I thought it might be worth being bound. Just to do something, *anything* rather than hide in the shadows.

"I'm going to come back," I said. "As soon as I've told Benedar everything. We can't just abandon the otherworlders.

"Let's face it, the Breaker is going to bind me

anyway. He's been threatening it ever since I came here yesterday. I'd rather confront him than wait in fear until he seeks me out."

Alanna opened her mouth. I never found out if she was going to agree with me or argue with me, because we were interrupted by Nadin.

He appeared in the connecting archway, slightly out of breath, as if he had run to get here.

"You," he said, pointing in my direction with an expression of annoyance. "Somehow I knew I'd find you here."

I stared back at him defiantly.

"I wish I could go back to yesterday evening and choose a different unit to repair the door," he said, shaking his head.

"What's the problem?" I asked when he showed no sign of continuing.

"I don't even know where to start. My master came back from a meeting of the elders just now, and he's using those crazy words from yesterday that I thought you were just making up.

"He says that the Breaker is going to drown another world so that it will belong to Imbera. The world that boy and girl come from. Then he is going to test their magic. We have to stay inside no matter what we hear. The other elders wanted to watch. My master isn't happy."

"He's never happy," Alanna pointed out. Nadin ignored her and carried on speaking.

"And *now*, the boys who did the repair with you are in the square. They want to know if you've been bound or not. There's a small Thinker with them. It doesn't matter what I say to get them to leave. He ties my head up in knots with arguments."

I smiled to myself. That sounded like Benedar. I made to go, but Nadin raised his hand.

"That's not even the worst of it."

I exchanged a glance with Alanna. What did he mean?

"They went to the edge of the island just now. To try to touch the Flyers, apparently."

Nadin's face showed how ridiculous he thought this was.

"But they didn't do it," he went on. "They say that four strangers appeared on the rock out of nowhere. And now the strangers are coming here."

17 The Initiation Word

It took me a moment to realise what must be happening.

"Appeared out of nowhere?" Alanna was saying. "What are you *talking* about?"

"More otherworlders!" I said excitedly. "Come to rescue Shannon and Jax!"

She looked back at me. I could see in her eyes a reflection of the same hope that I was feeling. It rose inside me, bright and eager, despite the fact that I knew the chances of success were small.

Four new magicians. Could the Breaker fight that many? Could the Binder really capture all four at once? I didn't know the answer, but I decided that I had to do everything I could to help them.

"I'm going to find them," I said determinedly. "I'm going to warn them about the Initiation Word."

Alanna nodded.

"Yes. Maybe they can use one of these spell things to protect themselves."

"Can I let them in through your master's house?" I said, turning to Nadin. "Your door will still be open, won't it? Like yesterday?"

His eyes were wide with fear and confusion.

"I don't... If I'm caught... What is an otherworlder?"

"The strangers are magicians from another world too," I said impatiently. "Like Jax and Shannon, the boy and girl who broke the door yesterday."

He gaped at me. He had obviously not considered that others might come as well.

"They can create doorways out of this magic they have. Portals. That's how they came to Imbera."

I raised my eyebrows in question.

"Well? Will you help?"

He was still lost for words.

"Take this," said Alanna. I glanced down to see that she had put a large gold-coloured key in my hand. It had sharp edges and was cold against my skin.

"Is this...?"

"Yes," she said. "It will open the large door. Then you don't need to waste time trying to get through Nadin's house unseen. His master is *very* observant."

Nadin looked relieved. But I wasn't so sure.

"What about you? If the Breaker finds out that you gave away the key to his house, what will happen then?"

"Don't worry about me. It's a small thing compared to what you're doing."

I was torn. There was no time, but I wished that I could tell her how much I admired her. It seemed like everyone was doing these brave, amazing things, when most of my day had been spent hiding and running from trouble.

"You can thank me when it's over," she said calmly.

I tried to copy her, but nervousness was making my breathing shallow.

"Al—alright," I replied, much less calmly. "I will."

Then I followed Nadin into his room and up the stairs.

We reached the entranceway unseen, but just as I was about to run for the door, he pulled me back. The faint sound of voices drifted down from one of the upstairs rooms, followed by laughter.

It was an unpleasant sound. The Opta were not naturally happy, despite their superior circumstances.

They were quick enough to laugh, usually at our expense, but it was a harsh, mocking kind of laughter.

"This could be it, Groven," came a girl's voice. "The breakthrough we've been waiting for. A way to escape this living death."

"Indeed. Thinker births are still high. The imbalance will just keep returning. Access to new magic is what we need. I would like to see it for myself, but Varun was insistent."

He paused. Then his voice became annoyed.

"I cannot wait for the day when we no longer depend on these recycled fools. They had their chance, and they made the wrong decision."

More laughter from the girl.

"You are *bad*, Groven. Not all of them had the choice, did they?"

There was the sound of a door closing, and I couldn't hear Groven's response.

I clenched my hands into fists, my rage making me forget what I was supposed to be doing. I didn't know what recycled meant, but I knew that I was one of the "fools".

When I glanced at Nadin, he had such a dejected look on his face that my anger faltered. I touched the key in my pocket. Anger wouldn't help me. I had to think clearly.

"Can we go now?" I asked in a whisper.

"Yes. The meeting went on late. They haven't eaten. They should stay upstairs for a while."

Once we were outside in the square, he

pointed to the shadows of a building in the opposite corner. I nodded my thanks and hurried to join the other boys.

I wasn't happy that Benedar had put himself close to danger, but he was so pleased to see me that it was hard to be cross with him. He could be so stubborn when he was trying to discover a new link.

He told me about the four strangers who were even now making their way through the city. Two boys and two girls. One pair nearly of binding age, like Albany, and one pair a bit younger, like me.

The strangers were not taking a direct route. They obviously did not know the island as we did. They had stepped onto the rock as if appearing from behind a wall. Except that there was no wall.

"They call it a portal," I said. "It's like a door, but it's made out of magic instead of stone."

Apparently the strangers were also generating a light source from their bare hands.

"A spell," I said, and Albany nodded.

"It's real," he replied in a low voice. "Magic. I've seen it for myself now. I believe it."

I tried to explain what I'd heard. About how many spells there were, and what they could do.

"The idea of a magic statue doesn't sound so crazy now," I added.

Benedar gasped.

"What?"

I looked quickly over my shoulder. I had my back to the square and was scared that he had seen something behind me.

"I didn't make the link before, but... If the four strangers aren't coming straight to the ruling house, then maybe they can't see the Flyers. And if they can't see the Flyers..."

"They can't be bound," said Alken. His spiky brown hair was still covered in rock dust from the night before. "And they might know if there *is* a spell inside that statue."

We exchanged excited glances. But then I remembered.

"No. The two otherworlders who came first, they are definitely bound," I said. "Why would these ones be any different?"

I had lost my audience. They were all staring at something. I turned to see two girls and two boys making their way across the square.

They were like us, but not like us. They walked with the same confidence as Jax, when I had first met him. Staring up at the Flyer, they paused for a moment.

There was a taller boy, whose brown hair was long and messy on top and almost shaved off underneath. It was strange. His expression was alert like a Thinker's. But he looked strong enough to lift rocks as well.

The taller girl had a silver symbol on her shoulder, like Jax. A different shape from his. Her hands were making a bright light that glowed above them.

It looked as if they were standing in their own personal sun. The dark red of her long hair showed up clearly.

The other boy, dressed in black, had a different symbol again. His hair was blond and straight, but it was his face that made me pause. He looked furious. So angry that you could see the magic energy radiating from him.

And then the second girl. Brown curls falling over her shoulders. Brightly coloured clothes. Some kind of paint around her eyes, which were glittering. No symbol.

The taller boy was now pushing at the door to the ruling house, obviously getting nowhere.

I showed the others the key that Alanna had given me and moved around the edge of the square until I was near the second girl.

I reached out to touch her arm. She jumped and spun round, ready to raise the alarm, but I put two fingers up to my mouth, and she managed to stay silent.

I showed her the key. She immediately understood and pushed the others out of the way. Before I put the key in the lock, I leaned closer to whisper my warning. I spoke fast.

"If he says the Initiation Word, you will be lost. She will bind you. It happened to your friends, and it could happen to you too. You *must* prevent him from speaking."

To my astonishment, she nodded calmly, saying that they knew about the Initiation Word already. She said they had a spell to stop it. I could hardly believe it.

"Our friends..." she added. "Are they still alive?"

"They are," I replied, explaining that the Opta leader wasn't done with the process yet. "But the boy, Jax, I fear he is already broken. I hope your spell can save him."

She hadn't expected this.

"*Broken?*" she repeated, as if she didn't understand the word.

There was no time to explain it to her. I had already taken too long. They might still be able to save Shannon. Hastily I turned the key in the lock.

"Go!" I said. "If he makes them submit to another round of symbols so soon, the girl Shannon will probably break as well. I doubt your spell works on me, so I will wait here. Shout for Cal if you need my help."

I stepped backwards out of the light and watched them enter. As the door opened wider, the sound of screaming could be heard. The Breaker hadn't wasted any time. I wondered if the portal was already open, letting Imbera's ocean pour into the world of Androva.

These otherworlders were strong. Were they strong enough? Part of me wanted to run after them and do whatever I could to help.

But it would be crazy. The Breaker would be spitting the Initiation Word at them right about now. I couldn't switch my ears off. And what if their spell didn't work? I had to wait.

Out of the corner of my eye, I saw Albany beckoning urgently to me. He had stepped out of the shadows and looked ready to come and get me if I didn't go to him.

Reluctantly I left the ruling house and returned to the others.

"*What happened?*" whispered Albany as soon as I was close enough. "Can they see the Flyers or not? Do they know if there's a spell inside that statue?"

Oh. I'd forgotten to ask them that. He rolled his eyes.

"Well, what *did* you talk about?"

"She said they knew about the Initiation Word. She said they had a spell to stop it."

"What?"

"How?"

"Does it work on us too?"

I shook my head at the barrage of questions.

"I don't know. We are not magicians, are we? Although…"

I remembered something Shannon had said.

"The Breaker told one of the otherworlders that the binding attaches to your force field. But she said that force field means magic. Not life."

Benedar was frowning.

"Force field, life essence, magic," he said. "If they turn out to be the same thing, we might all be magicians, and we don't even know it."

Alken and Sorvan scoffed. Albany half smiled and shook his head. Then his mouth opened in shock. What was he looking at?

It was Alanna. Stepping carefully out of the doorway of the ruling house. The light behind her meant that I could only see her in silhouette. Her expression was hidden.

"Wait here," I said to the others. "She might be bound or…"

Then I put my hand on Benedar's shoulder.

"Don't follow me." I glared at him. "I mean it. We can't lose you to the Gathering."

He didn't say anything. I ran across the square. If Alanna was brave enough to step outside the ruling house, then I could risk being seen as well.

"What is it?" I said, slightly out of breath.

"The first two otherworlders. They just came down the stairs, talking about closing the underwater portal. Neither of them are in a trance."

She grabbed my sleeve.

"Cal, I don't know what to do. Have they really beaten the process? If I'm wrong, and I go upstairs and I get bound... Kaylar will be all alone."

"I'll go," I said immediately. "I can tell them about the statue's eyes. They might be able to free us all."

"But..."

"The rest of my unit are over there. If anything happens to me, send Nadin to let them know."

I could hear raised voices coming from inside the ruling house.

"I'll be OK," I said, faking a confidence that I didn't have. "Anyway, you have to stay alive. Nadin told me you lead the information gathering."

I was through the doorway now.

"I'll come and get you when I know it's safe..."

I ran up the stairs before I could change my mind.

"... built on the deaths of others," came an angry voice. It was the girl with painted eyes.

"It's not something you can argue your way out of," she carried on. "It has to *stop*. How many people have you killed? Can you even remember?"

I hesitated behind the door.

"The Exta are not *people*." It was the Binder, her voice scornful. "The Exta are—"

I pushed the door open. Everyone stared at me. One second lasted forever.

The Breaker was on the floor. Unconscious. The Binder was injured, but still defiant. Fear was making me lightheaded.

I couldn't feel my legs properly, and I hoped I wasn't going to fall over.

"I don't care what you do to me," I said to the Binder, thinking of Benedar, Alanna, and the others. "But my brother deserves to live his life to its natural end."

Quickly I turned to the girl.

"Look to the creature on the roof. Its eyes change colour during the Gathering. The—"

"Medaxus!" said the Binder, almost singing the word.

The girl looked horrified.

How strange. I knew that word. Or did I?

"The... the... source of the... the... binding..."

My head was burning. *I want, I want, I want, I want. I'm going to die. I have to, I have to, I have to. Please, please, please, please.*

Kneeling. Begging. *Please, please, please. Yes, the*

symbols, yes, it's there, what I need, it's there, please, please. So close. Nearly...

18 The Fall Of The House Of Medaxus

Reaching. *Burning.* Pushed back. Shannon saying "No!"

Struggling against something. Someone. *I have to, I have to, let me, let me, please, please.*

Shannon again. Speaking. Smiling. Her hand. Glowing. Touching my arm.

Suddenly I could focus again. There was something cold inside my head, blocking out the burning. It was still there, but silent, as if pushed behind a wall. I blinked.

"What was I…?"

I tried to remember what I'd been saying to the other girl. She helped me, asking about the statue's eyes. Yes, I agreed, they changed colour.

"We are forced to watch from an early age, and recently we've been looking at the statue for clues about how the Gathering works."

"Oh no you don't," said the red-haired girl, suddenly and forcefully. As I watched, she used her magic to fold the Binder's sleeves tightly around her arms, until the symbols were hidden.

When I lifted my gaze to the Binder's face, I nearly laughed in shock. There was some more magic, in a horrible green colour, wrapped around her mouth. She was shouting angrily, but her words were completely silenced by it.

The girl with the painted eyes made a joke about it, like the Binder was nothing to her. I looked nervously at the Breaker on the floor, half expecting him to leap to her defence, but nothing happened.

Jax and the blond boy went outside to the statue. The rest of us followed, leaving the older boy and girl behind to watch the Opta leaders.

By the time we emerged into the square, Jax and his friend were already standing on top of the building. They had created a powerful yellow light that lit up the entire statue. I could hardly believe it. We'd been seconds behind them!

"How did they climb up there so fast?" I asked Shannon.

"Magic," she replied with a massive grin.

Her confidence was returning. Now that she was free from the Breaker, she was almost unrecognisable. Her eyes were glittering, and she was standing taller.

Jax said something about an Extraction Spell. He and the other boy lifted their hands, and the statue was surrounded with magic.

I wondered if I would ever get used to seeing it. These otherworlders took it for granted that they could just raise their hands and create energy to do whatever they wanted.

There was a noise like distant thunder. A grumbling and a groaning, getting louder and louder. Then it sounded like the statue was cracking. The Flyer roared.

I cringed, expecting that any moment doors would be flung open around the square, revealing Opta elders demanding to know where the noise was coming from.

Then I remembered what Nadin had said. Stay inside no matter what. That's what the Breaker had told them.

How brilliant. The Opta elders in the square would be listening to this demonstration of magical strength and congratulating themselves. Thinking it would soon be theirs. Not realising that it might be the sound of their own downfall instead. Maybe. Hopefully.

I glanced to where I knew Benedar and the others were hiding. I had felt the power of the Initiation Word for myself. I couldn't remember the actual word, thanks to Shannon. But I remembered the burning. It was impossible to resist. We weren't safe yet.

To my horror, as I looked, Benedar ran up to me. I told him off, keeping my voice low although I wanted to yell at him. My words were useless. It was too late, and he wasn't listening anyway.

He looked at Shannon and the other girl.

"Are these the otherworlders?" he asked innocently.

"Yes, we are," said the girl.

I gritted my teeth. As if he didn't already know the answer to that, and a lot more besides. All I needed was for Alanna to appear, and the two people I cared about the most could be bound within minutes.

The magic that had emerged from the Flyer's mouth was bright red, with stripes of orange and yellow. It swirled in the air, hissing angrily. We could see the spell now, streaming from the magic in a never-ending wave of energy.

"You must be Cal's brother," said Shannon. "I've heard all about you."

"I love my brother," said Benedar, and my heart clenched. I didn't know if I hated him or loved him.

Shannon touched my arm, as if she knew what I were thinking.

A minute later, I thought I'd stepped into a

dream. The glittering in her eyes expanded until her whole body was covered. And then she flew. She rose up to the statue as if she had invisible wings on her back. After a quick conversation, the other boy came down.

He told me his name. Darius. And the girl with painted eyes was called Penny. I introduced myself and Benedar, like we were meeting at the Book Rooms, calm as anything. When I'd just seen Shannon and Darius fly. *Fly*.

By the time I looked up again, Shannon and Jax had turned to the red magic. I hadn't seen them move the door to the ruling house. But it must have been like this.

Together, hands joined, her magic being controlled by him. As they had described to the Breaker. The best of them both. United against the evil spell.

It put up a fight, but in the end it disappeared in a small puff of air. Gone.

Shannon and Jax returned to the ground, telling the others that the spell had dissolved. I couldn't take my eyes off the Flyer. It looked as solid and menacing as ever.

"You mean we're free? Really, really free?" I said. I wanted to believe it. So much.

Jax said something about giving it a few days, but nodded. "No more Gatherings," he added, looking relieved. I wanted to feel relief as well, but I still worried it was only a dream. I'd had some crazy ones recently, after all.

The older boy and girl emerged from the ruling house, with puzzled expressions. Before they could explain, Penny interrupted.

"Jax and Shannon just killed the Medaxus enchantment, so I think we're pretty…"

She put her hand over her mouth and turned to me.

"I didn't think, I shouldn't have said that word! I'm so sorry, are you OK?"

And actually, I was. I could feel it, the end of the spell, trying to burn back into life inside me. But, like an echo, every time it tried, it was fainter. I reassured her.

I looked at Benedar. He screwed up his small nose.

"It tickles inside my head!" he said. "It's… oh. It's gone."

Right after that, he did something amazing. He looked up at the sky and told us that there were no more Flyers. I stared into the blackness until my eyes started to water, but I couldn't see any Flyers either. It was then that I started to believe.

I hugged him. It was the first time I ever had, and he hugged me back as if he never wanted to let me go.

"The dragons weren't real then?" asked Penny, sounding ever so slightly disappointed.

Of course. Shannon and Jax said they had followed the dragons. But they meant the Flyers.

The older boy was speaking again. He asked us to follow him back inside the ruling house.

It was a sight I had never thought to see. The Breaker and the Binder, broken themselves. Cringing, muttering, *tame*. Their symbols had vanished. Along with their sanity. Or so it seemed. I would hardly have known them.

"It was like something snapped behind their eyes," said the older boy. "Now they're like this. All he can say is *that word*," he added, with a careful glance in my direction.

"Medaxus?" I said cheerfully. "*That* word?"

He grinned. "That's the one. I take it you broke the spell then?"

"We did," said Jax. "The Exta are no longer at a disadvantage. Although they might actually have the upper hand, if half of the population has turned into that."

He pointed at the Binder and the Breaker. They didn't notice.

"Shame really," Jax went on. "I was looking forward to getting my own back, but I can hardly fight someone who doesn't even know who I am."

I felt the same. I was sure that the rest of my unit would too. Then I realised what Jax had said.

"Not half," I corrected.

"What?" Shannon said.

"Only one in ten are Opta."

She was shocked. "Wow. Then I guess you get to take your world back."

I shook my head. "Not the world. Just this city. But right now, that's enough for me. For us," I added, smiling at Benedar.

Then they had some kind of discussion about a misunderstanding between Jax and the older boy, whose name was Andy. It was soon straightened out, with a lot of laughing and joking between the six of them. The older girl with the red hair was called Valentina.

Jax called Shannon his girlfriend. He kissed her in front of everyone, quickly and confidently. He had obviously given a lot more kisses than I ever had.

Did that mean Alanna was *my* girlfriend? My cheeks became hot as I considered it. Was there such a thing as a *boy*friend too?

Suddenly I was desperate to see her. I was about to speak up, when the otherworlders said they had to return to Androva. The spell that had captured Jax and Shannon was hurting other magicians on their own world.

It seemed that this was not the first time a portal had been opened between Androva and Imbera.

They promised to come back. They left

happily, trying to be quiet, and I wondered how many Opta and Exta would see them. I realised that it wasn't my problem.

I sent Benedar to get Albany, Alken, and Sorvan. Then I turned to the door that led underground. Before I could reach it, it swung open.

Alanna stepped forward, slowly.

"Am I dreaming?" she said, giving me a wary look.

"Medaxus," I replied with a grin.

"What?"

"That's the Initiation Word."

She gasped in horror and backed away from me.

"No!" I said quickly, kicking myself for being so thoughtless. "No, it's OK… It doesn't work anymore. I promise. The otherworlders destroyed the spell."

I reached for her hand.

"Listen… Medaxus, Medaxus."

I spoke softly.

"It has no power over us. We're free."

"Medaxus," she repeated cautiously. Then more loudly. The third time, she stepped properly into the entrance hall. She looked up to the roof and raised her arms.

I was grinning. Our invisible chains had gone. I felt like reaching skywards as well.

"MEDAXUS!" she shouted.

Then she looked at me.

"Where are they?"

I glanced at the stairs. Within a second she was running up them, and I followed as fast as I could. I knew she was probably more capable than I was of defending herself, but that didn't mean I couldn't be there to help.

The Binder and Breaker were huddled where we'd left them. Eyes staring like dead fish. Mouths slack, now that the muttering had stopped. Arms and legs relaxed, as in sleep.

Alanna stood over them. Her whole body was trembling with anger. She bent over the Breaker, and grabbed hold of his chin, turning his face in her direction.

She waited a few seconds, but his vacant expression didn't change.

"I *despise* you," she said quietly and forcefully.

She released his chin, none too gently, and his head scraped against the stone wall.

"The game is over, *Varun*." Her mouth twisted. "You're in a trance just like your victims. Maybe you'll come out of it. Maybe you won't. But either way, *you've lost*."

She tugged the black-and-white ribbons from her hair. It fell past her shoulders, just as shiny as the first time I saw it. Then she threw the ribbons on top of his head like they were a piece of garbage she couldn't wait to get rid of.

She was the most impressive thing I'd ever seen. If the Breaker had been in his right mind, he'd have been furious. It almost made me hope he'd recover, just so he could receive her contempt knowingly.

As she turned back to me, we heard a noise from downstairs. The other boys had arrived. A quick look out of the window confirmed that the square was still empty.

I suppose that's the danger of having absolute authority, like the Breaker. If you tell everyone to stay away, there's no one to come running when you're in trouble.

"Cal!"

Albany. I walked with Alanna to the top of the stairs. Albany, Alken, and Sorvan were standing nervously in the doorway, and Benedar was trying to drag them forwards.

"Hey," I said. "Up here."

Albany looked up.

"Benedar's not making any sense. He says the Breaker is… broken? Did you hit him with rocks or something?"

"Now there's an idea," muttered Alanna.

"No," I said, laughing. "The otherworlders broke the spell. The Medaxus enchantment. And that broke him."

"Medaxus? What's that?"

"The Initiation Word."

He stepped back, and so did the others, fear in their eyes.

"It doesn't work anymore," I said reassuringly. "Believe me, you'd know if you were bound. It's like being on fire."

Alanna touched my hand.

"You were bound?" she said softly.

I nodded.

She looked at me with new respect. I stood a bit taller, and then I felt guilty, realising I probably didn't deserve it. I'd only been half-bound, after all. I'd never connected with the Binder's symbols.

The others still looked anxious, as if expecting disaster to strike at any moment. Benedar, exasperated, shouted Medaxus at them until they gradually stopped flinching.

"It's not going to hurt you!" he exclaimed. "It's like I said, the ruling house isn't in charge now. The House of Medaxus is powerless."

"The *House* of Medaxus?" I repeated.

"Yes. The symbols over the doorway. I just linked them. Now I know the word Medaxus, I used the s and the u and the e to figure out House."

I frowned.

"What is it?" said Alanna, but before I could answer, an Opta pushed his way confidently into the entrance hall. Maybe the Breaker had a friend after all.

19 Two Warnings

White tunic, white trousers, white shoes. Perfectly clean. Announcing to everyone that he did nothing all day.

Years of training had the boys hastily stepping aside. All except Benedar. He dug his small feet into the floor and stayed where he was.

The Opta, whose white hair was brushed straight back, flared his nostrils as if he were smelling rotten vegetables.

"Move," he said dismissively.

"No."

An incredulous look. Several, actually. Not just from the Opta, but from the rest of us as well. Benedar had rushed headlong into a test of our new freedom. The Opta recovered quickly.

"You might think this is what bravery feels like," he said to Benedar with a sneer. *Groven.* I recognised his voice.

"But," he went on, "it is actually stupidity.

Stupidity feels, looks, and sounds *exactly* like this."

Benedar gave a mischievous grin.

"No," he said again.

Groven raised his hand to hit Benedar. I scrambled to get down the stairs. Albany threw off his shock just in time to block the punch. He stood in front of Benedar with his fists raised.

I was at the bottom of the stairs now, ready to help. I could sense Alanna just behind me. But Albany didn't need us.

Whatever skills Groven took during the Time of Assignment, they weren't enough to beat a furious seventeen-year-old who'd spent most of his life carrying rocks. Groven stepped back almost immediately, one hand held to a swelling eye.

Then his other eye noticed me. His lip curled in a superior smile.

"Cal. I might have known. We can never quite keep you out of trouble, can we? No matter how dull the Worker programme assigned to you."

What was he talking about? He knew me!

"It is of no consequence. I'm sure the Breaker won't mind me sending you back early. And your little friends too."

He was making no sense. He smirked to see my confusion. Then his eye narrowed.

"Medaxus," he hissed.

I think we all held our breath. What if it were different when an Opta said it?

No. It wasn't. I knew almost immediately, because I knew what it felt like when it worked.

"Medaxus?" I said, walking up to him. "Is that what you said, Groven?"

His mouth opened and closed, but no sound came out. He stepped backwards.

"We can't hear you," I said, my anger rising. "Do you want to try again?"

He looked towards the stairs.

"Varun!" he shouted.

I grinned. At least, it was supposed to be a grin. But Groven shrank back as if I'd snarled at him.

"Varun!" he repeated, sounding desperate.

"Sorry," I said insincerely. "I think he's broken. Like the Initiation Word."

Groven stared at me. His arrogance was sliding off him. The face underneath was afraid. He was an enemy who had lost the ability to fight.

"Do you know what magic is?" I asked.

"You... you have no... where did you hear that word?" he faltered.

"You know it, then. Do you have it? I mean, are you a magician?"

Another stare.

"Answer me, Groven. Do the Opta have any

magic outside of the Medaxus enchantment?"

I couldn't read his expression. He lowered his hand, and I saw that his other eye was nearly swollen shut.

"How are you doing this?" he asked. "How?"

"Answer the question," I said.

Albany lifted his fist again, and Groven cowered slightly.

"No one is a magician anymore. Except for the Breaker and the Binder."

"Anymore? What does that mean?"

"The Medaxus enchantment is all that remains. Or was. If we can't bind you, then it no longer..."

His voice trailed off. From one second to the next, his fear magnified, turning his pupils large and black. His breaths came faster.

I felt no sympathy. Just curiosity about what was scaring him. Benedar was the only one who showed anything like concern.

"Help me to make the link," he said gently. "And then maybe we can do something about it."

Groven pressed his lips together. Benedar carried on.

"If there's no binding, and no breaking, then there's no Gathering. If there's no Gathering, then there's no Time of Assignment. If there's no Time of Assignment, there are no allocations..."

He put his head on one side.

"What happens to the Opta then?"

Groven shook his head.

"Do you die?" asked Benedar.

I felt my stomach twist. Did I want that? I wasn't sure. Now that I was free, would their deaths make my life any better?

Groven breathed in slowly.

"Death..." he said, "is coming for all of us."

I wanted to laugh. To deny his words as a poor attempt to scare us too. But the denial got stuck on my tongue.

Benedar stood his ground.

"How long can you survive without another allocation?"

"Longer than you."

He was looking at Albany.

"*What?*" Albany said scornfully. "We don't need allocations to survive, even if you do. Our lives are stolen. Were stolen, I mean. Once that stops..."

Groven was mastering his fear, taking advantage of Albany's confusion. He gave a bark of laughter.

"Do you know what a symbiotic relationship is, Exta?"

Albany scowled.

"No, and I don't care either. I could give you a punch every time you talk down to me though. How would you like that?"

"That's impossible," Benedar was saying, looking worried. "There is no symbiosis between the Opta and the Exta."

"What does it mean?" I asked him.

"It means that the relationship, the dependency, goes both ways. But how?"

He looked up at Groven.

"How?"

"No. Explaining it to you won't save my life. So why should I?"

He turned to me.

"Do you remember anything else apart from my name this time?"

Enough. He was almost in control again. I turned my back on him and spoke to the others.

"We shouldn't delay any longer. Let's tell everyone. Start with our list of informers. Maybe we can meet in the square tomorrow morning to agree what happens next."

Alanna nodded.

"I'll tell everyone here. The sooner we can stop being servants the better."

She reached up to whisper in my ear.

"Remember that the otherworlders said they'd come back. I heard them."

Then she spoke normally.

"The Opta might be all out of magic. But they're not."

I grinned. She was right. But why had she

whispered the first part? Then I got it. None of the Opta knew about the four rescuers from Androva. Well, except for the Binder and the Breaker, but they weren't exactly going to tell anyone.

It couldn't hurt to keep that to ourselves for a while longer. It might come in handy.

I glanced back at Groven.

"You'd better tell the other Opta. They're in for a shock. They can shout Medaxus from the rooftops, but they'll only be embarrassing themselves."

He glowered at me.

"Oh," I added, "you should check on the Binder and the Breaker as well. We're not going to look after them. And they're in no fit state to look after themselves."

Talking to an Opta without fear. I could get used to this.

Albany gave me a curious look. In the bright light of the ruling house, I could see his freckles more clearly than usual.

"What is it?" I said.

"You. The way you're changing. You could be a leader."

I blushed, suddenly feeling like a fraud. I was no leader.

"You see it too?" asked Benedar. "It's about time."

I laughed in disbelief.

"I'm going to pretend I didn't hear that. Can we get moving now?"

We split up, spreading the word one unit at a time. We left the square to Alanna. I wished I could be there when she told Nadin. What would he say to Groven now that he could say whatever he liked?

Sorvan returned to our unit to tell Maxen, Randall, and Beck. I was actually quite impressed that Maxen had stayed away. He must have been imagining the worst, because the others had been gone for ages.

Albany went to Haylen's unit first. I knew that it was Landra he really wanted to see. I was glad for him. And a bit envious. I'd only kissed Alanna once, and it didn't look like I was going to get another chance any time soon.

Benedar and I stayed in the city centre. We'd agreed that the childstation could wait until the morning. I don't know how the others found it, but it was way more difficult than I'd expected. Not one single person believed us straightaway.

I quickly realised that there was no point mentioning spells and magic. They were already looking at me like I might have lost my mind. Using words that sounded like gibberish to them wouldn't help.

It turned out that there was an easy way round

their doubts. All I had to do was find the nearest Opta and say "Medaxus" right in their face. The reaction that this created never failed to impress the watching Exta. They believed me then.

Taking the Opta weapon and using it against them… was it bad that I kind of enjoyed it? It's not like I was binding them, after all.

I hesitated outside Mordra's house. She had spared me the previous day. She knew me, just like Groven, but she'd let me go. If she had said the Initiation Word, I would not have been able to tell the otherworlders about the statue at all.

Her house Exta were asleep. We woke them carefully. Desperate for us not to disturb their masters, they covered our mouths when we started to explain.

There were chattering voices outside by this time. The streets were filling up with excited Exta. But these two remained unconvinced, shrinking back into a corner of their underground room.

"Wait here, then," I said. "Let me show you that your masters are no longer in charge."

I went upstairs. The lights were still on. The house was constructed in the same way as all the rest. A grey stone box, straight walls and perfect corners. Small square windows. Way too much space for the two Opta that lived there.

The entranceway ceiling stretched up to the

height of the house. There were three floors. Each had two rooms, running the length of the house on opposite sides.

A staircase zig zagged up to each floor. I started to climb. Benedar watched me. I tried to behave the same as I had for all the other houses we'd visited.

The first floor was empty. So was the second. Before I could touch the door to the third, it opened in front of me.

"Cal," Mordra said. Her pale eyes were anxious.

Just like with Groven, all I really knew was her name. Nothing else.

"Mordra," I said.

I heard a faint gasp, and a *"What?"* from Benedar.

She sighed.

"I was expecting you. "

"I… You were expecting me?"

She nodded.

"Whenever your memory returns, something like this happens. But it always leads to an early binding."

Her anxiety increased.

"I don't want to be the one to do it this time. You have to leave."

She started to turn away, but I grabbed her arm. It was thin, and I could nearly fit my whole hand around it.

"Medaxus," I said.

She slowly raised her other hand to her mouth.

"Noooooo…" she breathed.

"Yes," I said firmly. "You couldn't bind me even if you wanted to. I need you to tell your Exta that they can't be bound either."

I started pulling her down the stairs, gently but insistently.

"But Cal! What have you done?"

I ignored her, but she carried on, her voice rising.

"Cal! What have you done? How much do you remember? If the House of Medaxus has fallen for the second time, it will not rise again!"

I tripped, and fell down the last three steps. Pain exploded in my knees, and I nearly cried out.

The House of Medaxus. That's what Benedar had said, right before Groven barged in and distracted us. The words sliced through my head with more intensity than any of the memories so far.

Two chairs. No, *thrones*. Furnishings covering the grey stone. So many colours. The symbols over the entranceway. I could *read* them.

The House of Medaxus. Bound to serve our people until death, a promise never to be broken.

I struggled to my feet and looked at Mordra.

"What do you mean, the second time?"

"How do you know him?" added Benedar. He turned to me. "How does she know you? How do any of them know you?"

20 Creating A New City

There were no answers. Underneath the fantastical memory fragments, my mind was just the same old Worker fog. Mordra kept her mouth shut, seeing that we knew almost nothing.

Her Exta stepped into the street with hope in their eyes. Despite the sense of unease I was feeling about Groven's and Mordra's warnings, I decided to continue to the next house, and the next. We could hardly stop, anyway. Too many Exta knew by now.

Groven and Mordra could have been faking to scare us. That was the kind of thing an Opta would do. But somehow I knew they weren't. And I could see that Benedar was thinking and thinking, even while we were delivering the life-changing news.

There was a small line of concentration between his eyebrows, underneath his hair. He usually only got that when he was really distracted about some new link.

I drew him to one side.

"There will be time to figure it out later," I said to him. "We're not going to die tomorrow, are we?"

He considered this and then shook his head.

"So it can wait," I went on. "There are things to decide first. Now that we can choose for ourselves, I mean. We still have to keep the city running, after all. We all need food, water, somewhere to live. Maybe put the Opta in the caves?" I grinned. "And we'll take the houses?

"Not to mention how we deal with the Breeders and the childstation. We need Thinkers like you for that."

"And leaders like you," he said with a small smile.

"Stop calling me a leader," I said, rolling my eyes. "The world hasn't changed *that* much."

As it turned out, I was being a bit optimistic about making a new plan for the city. Other things got in the way at first.

As soon as everyone accepted their new freedom, the rage that rose up against our Opta oppressors was swift and impossible to stop. Groven's black eye was only the beginning. There was no mercy for those who had shown none.

The Exta had no magic, but fists and boots could inflict as much damage as a spell when the wearers of the boots were as angry as this.

I could understand it, even if I didn't participate. I would probably have enjoyed giving the Breaker a kick in the ribs with no fear of retaliation.

But I was worried about the time passing and distracted by those memories. Assuming they *were* memories and not a sign that I'd lost my grip on reality.

Benedar told me they were real. There were too many links for them to be otherwise, he said. I could sense that spiraling clock again, just like when I had lost Garrett. Except this time I didn't know how long we had left.

Together with some of our original informers, we put together a group of ten. We wanted a balance of Thinkers and physical strength, to give us the best chance of restoring calm to the city.

Benedar and I. Alanna. Albany and Alken. Haylen and Landra, who was just as tough as Albany in a fight.

A Thinker called Orman who worked in childstation assignments. He'd seen every single skill on the Opta list. Put together with our ten-digit identifier, he could look up strengths and weaknesses for anyone.

Jenner, a Thinker from energy allocation. She knew all of the other Thinkers who managed the city's resources, from food and water to technology.

And finally, Deera, a Worker from Jenner's unit. She maintained machinery. Anything that used the energy allocated by Jenner. If she couldn't fix it, she knew someone who could.

The ten of us worked fast to recruit the additional knowledge and strength to carry out our plan.

It took a little while to break through the chaos, but eventually we managed to gather all of the Opta together in the houses in the central square. It was more cosy than they were used to, but that was the least of their problems.

Then we presented our ideas to the other Exta. First, the Opta would be punished. The Thinkers had all agreed this was necessary. Otherwise the anger would never lessen.

The Opta would be moved to the worst of the caves. The ones where my unit had lived, to be precise. They'd be stripped of their fancy possessions and home comforts.

We would allow them to keep their clothes, but they'd never be pure white again. Most were already covered with bloodstains. Those Exta fists and boots had done a lot of damage. And seeing the white gradually disappear under a layer of dirt would be a satisfying reminder of their change in status.

We would celebrate. Another necessary part of

the plan, I'd been told. A way to mark the occasion before the creation of a new city. Freedom to eat, to explore, to make friends, and move on from the past.

Then a new reality. The Opta would be put to work. They'd been shocked enough by the hostility to do what we wanted. At least for now.

They couldn't do it all, though. Even after we'd scrapped all of the unnecessary tasks. We would each have to contribute.

But it would be fair, and much, much easier than what we'd been used to. There would be rest days. We could talk to each other. We could learn how to be happy.

Orman said the plan would probably change a lot before it worked. He said there was no way to predict individual behaviour and we'd be crazy to try.

Benedar agreed.

"But change is good," he said, his thin face lighting up with a smile. "You can discover new links every five minutes if things are allowed to change."

My role as leader was becoming a standing joke between me and Albany. No matter how I tried to sidestep the attention, everyone seemed to look to me for advice and to make decisions.

"I know less than anyone!" I protested. "I'm a buildings Worker. I know rocks, ladders, and hammers. That's *all*."

Albany just laughed.

"If that's what you really think, you're kidding yourself Cal. You risked your own life to tell the otherworlders how to defeat the Medaxus."

"And," said Benedar, "leaders aren't supposed to know everything. Leaders convince the rest to follow, so that stuff gets done. *That's* all."

He grinned as he repeated my words back to me.

I wasn't comfortable with it, but there didn't seem to be anything I could do to make it go away. Besides, there was no time to argue.

Now that we had a basic plan to make our lives work, we needed to understand the rest of it. The breeding station. The childstation. And that room underneath the ruling house.

The Opta refused to talk. Actually, that's not completely true. The Breaker and the Binder babbled all day long, but the nonsense that came out of their mouths was of no use to anyone.

The other Opta watched us in silence. They were compliant enough, but obviously waiting for something to happen. It was quite unsettling, not that I would ever admit that to anyone.

Jenner said the underground room used more energy than anything else in the city. Like all of the Thinkers, she was excited and overwhelmed by the amount of information she was now able to access.

"All those boxes… they're switched on, all the time. They're constantly using power."

Her blue eyes were squinting slightly with tiredness, but it didn't seem to be affecting her enthusiasm.

"We need to know what's inside the boxes. The Time of Assignment happened just before the otherworlders arrived. Which means that the boxes should be empty. We think. But they're still using so much power."

I remembered what Alanna had said about the second container. We decided to check it after figuring out the breeding station and the childstation. Actual living Exta were more important than white boxes.

The two places where Exta were born, and then spent the first six years of life, were cut off from the rest of the city. If an Exta joined them as a Worker or a Thinker, that was it. They never came out.

Well, not until the time came for their own private Gathering, of course. This happened once their age and skills had progressed enough, and a new younger brother or sister had been identified to replace them.

We started with the childstation. I only had vague memories of my time there. Playing. Then learning. Until finally, absolute obedience. But as

I walked into the entrance room, I found that I remembered a lot more.

This was where I had first met Garrett. And Benedar. So young and optimistic the first time. So bitter and angry the second.

Desks in rows. Chairs neatly stacked. A machine like the ones used by many Thinkers in the corner. Nothing to show that children ever came here.

It was deserted. There had not been any younger brother and sister collections for days. The Thinkers that usually scheduled them had been too busy exploring their new freedom.

After a moment's hesitation, I pushed open the doors to the hallway. Silence. No locks to keep them in. Or us out. Yet no one had dared to open them.

I walked faster, starting to worry. Surely there ought to be some noise? Some evidence of the scraps that lived here?

We found them all outside. There was a kind of central space enclosed by the walls of the childstation building so that the children could go outside yet remain separate from the city. They had to make sure we saw the Flyers. And learned to fear them.

It was also a place to test and develop certain skills, like cultivation or building. It was mostly dark of course, but still better than being inside all the time. We'd been allowed to draw on the grey stone and grow pretty leaves to add flavour to our dried fish.

The scraps were lined up quietly in rows, and Workers were handing out bowls of water from the fountain. They didn't notice us at first.

"That's right, one at a time. The food will come later. The supplies get interrupted sometimes—it doesn't mean anything."

I recognised the girl talking. Vella with the grey eyes. So did Benedar.

"Vella!" he called, and dodged past me to run and hug her. She jumped with the shock, even as she automatically put her arms around him. I could see her lips mouthing his name, her brow furrowed in confusion.

Then she noticed the rest of us, and froze. Everyone caught her fear almost immediately, like a gust of wind had blown it from person to person.

I felt bad for them, and hurried to offer reassurance. It helped that we had Haylen with us too. They remembered her and Benedar and were quickly convinced when we told them what had happened.

Most of them had noticed the absent Flyers. We didn't need to provide any of the crazier-sounding details about magic and spells. They believed it was different now.

The Workers were beyond delighted to know that the scraps they looked after weren't going to be bound. We checked, but there seemed to be nothing joining the childstation to the breeding station. No connection that we should be fearful of breaking.

We encouraged them to leave their prison boundaries and get themselves food and drink from the city nearby. The older scraps were quick to agree, which forced their Workers to be brave and follow.

I hoped it would soften the anger that remained. The children didn't hate the Opta the way we did. They would be more interested in having fun than taking revenge.

There was a handful of new babies who'd arrived right after the Time of Assignment. This was normal practice. The Breaker took his life essences, and once they'd been allocated, new Exta were born to keep the total numbers the same.

I looked at these babies curiously. They couldn't know how changed their city was now. Nor did they care. They were only interested in being fed and having a warm pair of arms to hold them. And we had no plans to deny them this.

However, the babies ended up with something new after all. From the childstation we moved to the breeding station next door. Again, no locks.

But we were obviously the first to throw open the doors from this side.

This time the shock took far longer to overcome. The Workers on the other side barred our way, preventing us from reaching any of the Breeders that lived there. We did not want to use force. We tried to reason with them.

The raised voices became loud enough for one of the Breeders to hear us. It was a girl, not much older than me.

She ran into the hallway and then skidded to a halt. I glanced down, to see bare toes at the end of clean, small feet.

Her face was tearstained and exhausted. Her brown hair was tied severely back. Her eyes were desperate.

"You... the childstation... can I go there? If the Opta are defeated, can I go there? My baby..."

Suddenly she made a decision, before we could answer her. She pushed past us. More girls were appearing behind the Workers. Some looked like they had just woken up. Some of them had swollen stomachs.

I pulled a face, unable to prevent a feeling of... yuck. Babies. *Inside* the Breeders. Rather than think about this too much, I turned to follow the first girl.

I knew where she needed to be. I showed her

the room with the babies. She made a kind of choking sobbing noise and reached for one of them.

She lifted it and held it close, tears falling down her face. She was whispering to it.

"I'm your Breeder. Me. I'm going to look after you now. *I'm* your Breeder," she repeated fiercely.

"No," I said softly. She lifted her head and glared at me, but my expression didn't waver. I knew a different word. A better word.

"Not Breeder. Mother," I said.

We reunited all the babies with their mothers. All the tiny scraps less than one year old had girls in the breeding station who remembered them. Who knew their names, and cried fresh tears to see them again.

It almost made me wish… but no. I was too old. And I had no time to be sentimental. We still had to figure out the room underneath the ruling house.

In less than two weeks, after the usual Time of Assignment, more babies were supposed to be born. When the allocations were keyed in by Alanna, the life essences passed through a filter, and *something* travelled along a pipe to the breeding station.

Except that it would not. Not anymore. We had to discover its purpose. And then try to prevent any difficulty caused when it wasn't there.

That night, most of us finally slept properly, too exhausted to stay awake wondering and planning anymore. In the morning, Alanna and I went with Benedar and Orman to the underground room.

21 Memory Banks

The walk through the tunnel was longer than I remembered. Orman cracked his knuckles, and the sound echoed off the damp stone walls.

"What?" he said, when we all turned to look at him.

"Nothing," replied Alanna. "I was just thinking that we needed some weird noises. You know, to make this whole experience a bit scarier."

Benedar giggled.

"Glad I could help," said Orman. The corner of his mouth turned up in a half-smile. His dark hair was brushed straight back, and his eyebrows made a thick, straight line over across his brow.

It looked like he was frowning pretty much all the time. But now that I'd spent a few days with him, I knew that he was quite easy-going.

Alanna unlocked the door. I kept my eyes half closed until they adjusted to the bright light inside. The low, continuous humming noise was the same as before. The machine in the centre, however, was black and silent.

"Where shall we start?" asked Alanna.

Orman went straight to the machine, trying to switch it on. Alanna helped him. Benedar walked from one end of the room to the other.

"It's almost exactly like you described," he told me.

"Almost?" I said. "What did I get wrong?"

"There's a pattern to the boxes."

I looked at the white cubes, piled on top of each other in identical rows. I couldn't see any way to tell them apart.

"What pattern?" I asked, mystified.

He grabbed my hand, taking me to the far wall. To where my box was located.

"These boxes were first," he said.

"How do you know that? Zack said they could have been first *or* last."

"It's the arrangement of the cables and pipes. They start at the back, and new layers are added from there. Like we saw in the place where Jenner works."

I nodded. "OK."

"And, the boxes get more complicated."

I stared at the white rows again. All the boxes still looked exactly the same.

"How?"

He ran his hand over the top of the box with my identifier on it. I stiffened, expecting to feel something, but of course I didn't.

"This box, and this one"—he touched the one immediately to the right of it—"were the first. They're unique. The next boxes are slightly bigger. Look."

He took my hand and put it on top of the join between the boxes. He was right. I could feel the slight increase in size, even if I couldn't easily see it.

"It goes like that all the way to the door," Benedar said. "The last boxes are probably this much taller."

He held up his thumb.

"But the increase is so gradual, and the boxes so similar, that your eyes tell you they're the same."

"You know that's *my* box," I said.

"I guessed."

"So who is next to me? And why are we different from all the rest?"

He shook his head. "I can't answer the second question yet. But why don't we ask Alanna to look up the identifier on the other box?"

The machine was working. Alanna typed in the ten digits, and we waited for the flashing lines on the screen to return the answer.

Garrett.

Garrett and I. Next to each other. The same.

"Who's Garrett?" said Alanna.

"His older brother," said Benedar, looking sad.
Garrett and I.

I could hear the Breaker's voice in my head,
and the words he had spoken when Albany and I
had been forced to watch him at work.

*No matter the random instructions given to the
breeding programme, there is a reassuring pattern to life.*

I shook my head slightly to clear the memory.

"We need to understand how these boxes
work. And we need to find out how this place
links to the breeding station."

They nodded. I was only repeating what we'd
already agreed, after all. But I felt a new sense of
urgency that I couldn't explain. Time was not on
our side. I was more certain about that than ever
before.

We started with mine. If there was any risk to
doing this, it might as well be me that faced it.
Alanna showed us the second compartment. The
front of the box had a panel underneath the
identifier. It came off quite easily if pressed in the
right place.

She had discovered it by accident when she
was cleaning off the mark of a dirty fingerprint.
After that first time I was here.

She wasn't supposed to touch the boxes, but
she'd been more worried about the Breaker

seeing the evidence of our exploring.

The panel showed compartments 1 and 2, plus three symbols against each. Compartment 1 was empty. Compartment 2 had a light shining from the inside. The light was visible at the edges and behind some of the symbols. Different colours flickered within it.

"Do you know what these letters mean?" asked Benedar.

"No," said Alanna, slightly defensively. "I can't read. There are no Thinkers in the leaders' houses. I can use the identifiers, but that's all."

He touched the first symbols.

"This says Worker or Thinker. Compartment 2 has the Thinker part lit up."

He looked at me.

"If part of you is in there, then part of you is a Thinker."

I blinked in shock.

He moved to the second symbols.

"This says Physical or Cerebral. Compartment 2 has the Cerebral part lit up."

He raised his eyebrows at Orman. Then they turned to look at me.

"No, I don't know what ser-serry—whatever it is means," I said.

"It means the opposite of Physical. To do with the mind, the intellect," explained Orman.

"Huh," I said, feeling myself bristle. "No

surprise that part's locked inside a box, is it?"

Benedar rolled his eyes.

"If you'll let me explain, I was *going* to pay you a compliment. It tells us that there are types of Worker and Thinker."

I glanced at Alanna, but she looked as confused as I felt. Benedar carried on.

"A Physical Worker would be like you, Cal. Buildings repair. A Cerebral Worker would be more like Alanna."

He grinned.

"What you've done recently, without being a Thinker or Cerebral... You'll be a force to be reckoned with when you get it all back."

I lowered my gaze. Benedar's faith in me was great and everything, but I was afraid he'd be disappointed when he knew how ordinary I really was.

"And the third group of symbols?" I asked.

"Memories. That's what it says. And they're all in the second compartment."

I reached out to touch it. I wanted to fill the gaps in my memories so badly. I'd settle for being a Worker the rest of my life, if only I could remember everything.

For a few seconds, the light inside the box seemed to create an answering buzz inside my head. As I traced the light spilling from the edges, it felt a bit like the draw of a magnet.

I pulled my fingers back suddenly, not liking the sensation.

"What?" asked Benedar. "Did you feel something?"

"No," I lied. "Can we check a few more boxes? We should prove your theory before we do anything with it."

He looked at me suspiciously, but Orman had already started looking for his own box. After a glance at me, Alanna went to the machine to help.

"I know when you're lying, Cal," Benedar whispered. "Anyway, I saw something in your eyes."

My stupid eyes again. I opened my mouth to complain, but he stopped me.

"No, not like that," he said. "I mean your eyes changed colour."

"They *what*?"

"Changed colour. They went almost silver. Like…"

He stopped, and I waited, half scared and half excited.

"Like the otherworlders. Like magic."

My excitement turned to embarrassment. Hearing it spoken out loud made it sound ridiculous.

"No," I said, shaking my head. "No way. The magic is gone. Groven said so."

"Do it again," he said.

"No."

If I did it again and nothing happened, I knew that it would be a big let-down.

He grabbed my hand in his smaller one, taking me by surprise. He pushed my palm against the box, but the strange feeling didn't return.

"I said *no!*"

My disappointment made me angry. I pulled my hand away and glared at him.

"Tomorrow," he said calmly. "We'll try again tomorrow."

"Not if I have anything to do with it," I muttered.

The rest of the boxes we checked seemed to prove the rule about the symbols. And every single box had memories locked in the second compartment.

As the boxes got larger, there were more layers to the symbols. More possible combinations between the two compartments.

Then Orman and Benedar figured out the timing of the allocations. It was so much better than we'd feared. The Time of Assignment created new Exta life at the start of the breeding cycle, not at the end of it.

If the allocations stopped, the only effect would be that no more babies would start growing. And as there were no more Gatherings either, surely this was just a new balance?

We ate our evening meal feeling relieved. Jenner also had good news to share. She had recalculated the food and water distribution with some of the other Thinkers.

Without the amount that the Opta were accustomed to wasting, there would be plenty to go around. I was glad. More food would go a long way to keeping everyone happy.

Before going to sleep, I went for a walk to the edge of the island. I carried a handheld light, but switched it off after a little while, preferring to be alone in the darkness.

Whatever there was to fear on Imbera now, I didn't think it was going to come from the black sky. And the lack of light was soothing, after spending most of the day in that bright room.

I knelt down and splashed some water onto my face, glad of the coolness. Then I sat down to think about the buzzing in my head from earlier. I tried to get it back. The more I concentrated, the further away it seemed to be.

Eventually I stopped and leaned back against the rocks. I was pretty tired all of a sudden. When I closed my eyes, I could have fallen headlong into sleep if I'd allowed myself.

I thought I was dreaming when the buzzing returned. The feeling expanded inside my head and extended down my arms. My palms were tingling, like when I had touched the Flyer.

I lifted my eyelids slowly and raised my hands up off my knees. I just had time to notice that they were giving off a weak glow, when I heard a voice.

"Cal? Are you out here?"

It was Alanna. The buzzing disappeared, and the glow vanished like I'd flicked a switch.

I wasn't too disappointed. It had happened twice now. And there'd been no white box to help me this time. Pushing down a wave of excitement at the thought of actually possessing magic of my own, I got to my feet.

"I'm here," I called. "Near the water."

I heard her footsteps getting closer. I switched the light back on, and her shadow appeared in front of me.

"Hey," she said.

"Hey," I repeated.

She laughed.

"Are you OK?"

"Yes. I just wanted to think about something. Benedar has another crazy idea, and I think he's right."

"What idea?" she asked.

"There might be some magic left after all. Even without the otherworlders."

I could see her white teeth as she grinned. Before I could change my mind, I leaned forward to kiss her. My heart raced when she kissed me back. Her mouth tasted sweet, like the berries we'd just eaten.

The only noise was the sound of the ocean water lapping against the rocks. I closed my eyes. I could have kissed her forever.

I lifted my hands to her face, and she pulled away from me. Guiltily I stepped backwards, feeling my ankle turn over on the rock's uneven surface.

"How are you doing that?" she asked. She had one hand touching her cheek, and the other was pointing at me.

I looked down. My hands were glowing again.

"I—I'm sorry," I stammered.

She reached for me and pressed her palm to mine.

"Is this what it feels like? Magic?"

"I don't know. I think so."

"Then how…?"

I shook my head.

"I wish I knew. It happened when I touched the white box today."

"But we all did that," she argued. "And I don't know about the others, but nothing like this happened to me."

"Benedar thinks it must be linked to the strange memories and the fact that the Opta know who I am."

The glow was fading again. We discussed it some more on our way back to the city, but there were no obvious answers.

Benedar was waiting up for me, to tell me that another section of the Book Rooms had been unlocked that evening. He said there was a good chance some of the answers would be there.

But the following day, something happened before he could start reading. The otherworlders came back.

22 Tiredness Or Sickness?

I sat up groggily, feeling like I had only just gone to sleep. The room was lit up in shades of red and gold from the sun. Through the window of this fourth floor room, it looked like the sky was on fire.

The Opta had always kept their windows covered when the sun rose. Their white skin could not tolerate the sun at all.

I stretched, reaching my fingertips up towards the ceiling. Why was it so difficult to wake up this morning? Yes, I had stayed up late. But I hadn't spent the previous day carrying rocks. I shouldn't be feeling this tired.

I looked down at the bed, wondering if anyone would notice if I went back to sleep for a little while.

Then I noticed the clock. It was almost lunchtime! *What?*

A sudden wave of dizziness made me sit down

again.

"Cal?"

I had my back to the door, but I recognised Benedar's voice. The dizziness was subsiding, so I risked turning round.

"Yeah. Why didn't you wake me up?"

"We thought you… Cal, are you alright? You look terrible."

I stood up, determined to prove him wrong. My legs were a tiny bit shaky, but apart from that, I seemed to be recovered.

"I'm fine. I just… I guess I didn't sleep very well."

"You look like you haven't slept at all."

I scowled.

"Well thanks, little brother."

He smiled, but I could see that he was still worried.

I took a deep breath.

"I *am* fine. A bit of tiredness isn't going to kill me, is it?"

Slowly, he shook his head. Then he brightened.

"I came to get you because we've got some visitors."

"Who?" I asked.

"The otherworlders."

My enthusiasm broke through the strange tiredness. I was so glad they had kept their promise to return. Maybe they could tell me if I really was becoming a magician. Maybe they could get the white boxes to open.

"That's brilliant. Where are they?"

I reached for my boots and tried to flatten my curly hair. Unsuccessfully.

Benedar wrinkled his nose.

"We live indoors now, Cal. You don't *have* to walk around looking like you spent the night on the floor of a cave."

Sighing, I went to the bathroom. I still wasn't used to the idea of washing every day. When I saw my reflection in the looking glass, I hesitated.

I could see what Benedar had been talking about. There were purple smudges under my eyes. I rubbed at them, but they wouldn't go away.

Now my eyes looked nervous. I searched my mind for an explanation. Perhaps magic was hard work at first. That could be it.

When I was a bit cleaner, I joined Benedar at the top of the stairs.

"Where are they?" I asked him.

"Downstairs. It's getting a bit crowded. Everyone wants to meet them."

We were living in the ruling house. Alanna had overcome my resistance by telling me that she wanted to wipe out any trace of the Breaker and the Binder.

She said the best way to get rid of them was to make the house ours instead. Anyway, it was the only one big enough to take all ten of us, and we wanted to keep our new group together.

There were so many *things*. The biggest problem in an Opta's life was boredom. All that time on their hands, yet nothing useful to do.

After we moved in, we mostly ignored all their stuff. We were busy creating a new city. We didn't have time for games and amusements. And how many white dresses had the Binder needed anyway? Surely not *that* many.

There was one thing we hadn't ignored though. Once we'd understood what we had found, all of the buildings Workers, including me, had used every tool we had in order to destroy it.

My shoulders had ached that day. But it had been worth it. In every house in the city, we had smashed the very top room to pieces.

We hadn't known straight away. It was just a room, with a plain bed or two pushed against the wall, and a canopy. Then Jenner and Deera had recognised parts of the machine underneath it. Deera had repaired pieces of it before, in her workshop.

Jenner said it was a type of diffuser. Another word I didn't know. Apparently it was a machine that could expand and soften a supply of air. They had thought it was used for heating. To keep the Opta houses perfectly warm at all times.

When we ripped off the canopy, the sight of the clear pipe underneath it made me feel sick. I had seen it before. It was the kind of pipe that carried our life essences.

Benedar and Jenner figured out the links while the rest of us listened. Deera bit her lip until it started to bleed. There were tears on her blonde eyelashes.

Diffusers work on light as well as air. These rooms had been used during the Time of Assignment. Lives turned into rainbows, forcibly stolen and then consumed by the ancient white ghosts that had ruled over us.

Being confronted with the evidence had brought my anger into sharp focus. Our deaths were part of their *furniture*.

While I had destroyed the machine, I imagined my hammer connecting with the Breaker's face over and over.

If he'd been in front of me at that moment, I think I would have killed him. Whether he knew who I was or not.

And now the otherworlders were back. I had a lot to tell them. A lot to ask them about.

I followed Benedar down the stairs all the way to the entrance hall. Exta were spilling out into the main square, trying to catch a glimpse of our rescuers.

Jax and Shannon. Darius and Penny. I had made Benedar write down their names and repeat them to me so that I would be sure to remember. The older boy and girl, Andy and Valentina, had not returned.

"Cal!" said Shannon when she saw me, giving a big grin. Her lips were painted, red and shiny, and there were precise black lines drawn onto her eyelids.

Jax had one arm around her shoulders. His green eyes were glittering with a layer of silver that matched the colour of the star on his shirt.

I wondered how we could ever have thought they were Exta, even for a moment.

Shannon broke away from Jax and came to give me a hug. He watched us, not hostile exactly, but definitely more guarded than she was.

Penny and Darius were talking to Alanna. Albany and Landra were leaning closer to listen. Everyone else was staring. None of the otherworlders seemed remotely bothered by the attention.

I returned Shannon's hug slightly self-consciously. Suddenly the buzzing in my head started up again. I felt it pull me towards her ten times more powerfully than the white box had.

She went still.

"Sorry…" I said, drawing back.

She looked at me with eyes that gleamed silver.

"What on Earth is this?" she murmured.

I didn't feel tired anymore. Not even a little bit.

"Earth?" I repeated. "What's Earth?"

"It's where I come from."

"I thought that was Androva."

I didn't know how I was still talking. It was like I'd swallowed a battery and it was lighting me up from the inside.

"No," she said. "Androva is where Jax and Darius come from. Penny and I are from Earth. A different world entirely."

She was starting to smile.

"I thought you told me you weren't a magician?" she said.

I was leaning closer to her again.

"I'm not... Well, that is..."

"Shannon? What's going on?" said Jax abruptly. I hadn't noticed him walk over to us. He was looking at me and Shannon suspiciously.

"Cal is with Alanna," said Benedar from behind me.

We all spun round to look at him. He had his arms folded and was staring at Jax.

"You're making the wrong link," he continued pointedly. Jax hesitated for a moment and then relaxed.

"But what *is* going on?" he repeated.

"We were hoping you could explain that to

us," said Benedar. "We need to understand how magicians become magicians. Because it seems to be happening to Cal."

Before Jax could answer, Darius called over to him.

"Penny and I are going outside. Apparently there are a lot of Exta who have never seen what magic looks like. I thought we could show them a few spells."

He turned to Penny, who nodded enthusiastically.

"Sounds like a great idea," Jax replied. "We're going to stay here and talk to Cal and his, er, brother, about something."

He frowned at Benedar.

"For brothers, you don't look anything alike."

"Why would we?" asked Benedar, frowning back.

"Um, because you have the same parents?"

"Parents? What are parents?"

Benedar looked at me, but I hadn't heard the word before either.

"Your mother and father of course!" said Jax, slightly impatiently.

"Then mother and father, and parents, and Breeders are all versions of the same thing?" I asked.

"Well," said Shannon, looking uncomfortable, "parents do a bit more than just breeding."

The memory whispered to me again. Your father and I are very proud of you, she'd said. My mother.

Alanna had come to stand next to me.

"Why don't we take them to the underground room?" she said. "It's probably the best place to explain what Imbera used to be like."

By the time we'd finished, Jax and Shannon were both incredibly angry.

"Are you *sure* Varun's lost his mind?" said Jax through gritted teeth. "He could be faking it to avoid facing up to what he's done. A few Combat Spells might help him back to sanity."

His hands were glowing almost white. Shannon's too. I could feel their power. It made the air crackle with energy.

The Breaker must have thought all his Gatherings had come at once when he realised what they were capable of.

If their friends had not come to save them, both Imbera and Androva might now belong to the Breaker and the Binder.

"He's not the problem," said Benedar. "Now that his allocations have stopped, I'm certain that he will die sooner or later.

"The problem is what Groven and Mordra said about the House of Medaxus and how much time we have left."

"Benedar's right," I said. "Can you help us to

understand magic a bit better? Why is there magic inside my head now? And how can I use it?"

I had to stifle a yawn. I wished I knew how to switch the magic back on. Since stepping away from Shannon, I'd been feeling gradually more and more exhausted.

"I want to know how to get into the second compartment," said Alanna. "I want the rest of my skills back."

They nodded.

"We'll do whatever we can," promised Shannon. "But some of this is new to us as well. Combining technology with magic in this way"— she gestured to the boxes—"that's not what Androva does. Or Earth. Not yet, anyway."

"Earth?" said Alanna.

"My world." Shannon smiled.

She turned to the box behind her and asked Alanna to remove the panel. Then she took a small device from her back pocket and held it in front of her.

When I leaned closer, I could see an image on the screen of the device. It was an exact replica of the box in front of it. A machine with eyes? How was that possible?

Shannon froze the image several times, capturing the box from different angles. Then she stepped back and did the same with the rest of the room.

Jax held out his hands and projected magical energy from them. It surrounded the box, coating it in silver mist.

We watched in silence. I rubbed at my eyes, trying to get rid of the tiredness.

Soon there was a pattern within the mist. It was brighter along the edges of the second compartment, where it was touching the coloured light inside.

Then Jax turned his hands over and the mist vanished.

"There is some kind of spell inside," he confirmed. "I could probably draw it out if I tried. But I don't think I should.

"I'm not feeling the same connection you described," he added, looking at me.

"Which makes me think that it's not mine to take."

I wanted to say something intelligent, but the tiredness was like a heavy rock inside my head.

"Cal is sick," said Benedar.

"What?"

Alanna's voice.

Everyone was staring at me.

"I'm not sick."

I was struggling to push the words out of my mouth.

Benedar walked up to me and rested his small

hand on my arm.

"You're so tired right now that I could probably push you over," he said gently.

At his words, the room tilted around me. I *was* tired. So, so tired. Why was I so tired? The ceiling swam in and out of focus.

"Tip his head back."

Wait a minute, the *ceiling*? Why was I lying on the floor?

There was something dripping onto my lips. I tried to turn my head away, but someone held it easily in place, pushing my chin down so that the drops fell inside my mouth.

"It's a Portal Remedy," someone said. "It should wake him up."

It tasted like cold, clean water, yet it wasn't liquid. I opened my eyes and everything snapped back into focus. Shannon's hand above my mouth. Her nails were purple. There were silver droplets falling one by one from her fingertips. I swallowed.

She lifted her hand away, and I scrambled to sit up.

"Take it easy," said Jax, supporting me.

"What was that?" I asked.

"A simple spell to counteract tiredness," said Shannon. She smiled at me, but her eyes were anxious.

"I think your brother's right. You might be

sick."

23 Imbera As It Was

After I convinced them that I was back to normal, we went upstairs. They mixed some more of the remedy spell with a large bottle of water. I was to drink a small glass of it if the tiredness returned.

While they created the spell, Shannon told us she had a theory about where my magic had come from. She reminded me what the Breaker had told her. The Medaxus enchantment works on the force field.

She said that on Androva it was necessary to have contact with another magician to activate the first spark of magic. Without this, the force field has no centre and you cannot be a magician. Perhaps the Exta were like this too.

"You touched my force field," she reminded me. "If that created your spark, it would explain why you were drawn to me earlier. Our force fields will always have that connection."

Jax pressed his mouth into a line. His green eyes narrowed slightly.

"Always?" I asked.

She nodded.

"It was Jax's force field that activated my magic. We have a similar connection."

She smiled at Jax, and his expression softened.

"There are no magicians on Earth except for me and Penny. No one has a force field on our world anymore. It took a powerful reversing spell to reinstate them.

"But," she continued, looking thoughtful, "I think it's different for you. I think you all have force fields. You just didn't have contact with another magician to activate the spark."

"The Breaker was a magician," I pointed out.

"Somehow I doubt you'd have noticed the magic inside your head while he was torturing you," said Jax.

"And it usually takes a couple of weeks before you can see it. You'd have been... um... *gathered* by then."

Alanna was leaning forwards.

"I touched his magic, Cal's magic," she said. "Does that mean it will happen to me too?"

"Probably," Shannon replied.

Alanna gave me a look of excitement mixed with fear.

Jax seemed very happy all of a sudden. Oh. Of

course. He'd obviously prefer me having a connection to Alanna than to *his* girlfriend.

"Is that why I'm so tired?" I asked hopefully.

"No," said Shannon. "Unless Imberan physiology is different from ours."

"Fizz... What?"

"I don't think it is," said Benedar. "From what I've seen, we're very similar."

It sounded like my tiredness wasn't magic-related then.

Judging by the cheering coming from outside, Darius and Penny were still keeping everyone entertained.

Jax and Shannon got up, saying that they were out of time. They would try to come back the following week.

Androva was busy with some kind of celebration for what they called spring. It sounded like our Planting Season.

Shannon said one last thing to me.

"Whatever is in that compartment, it's obviously drawn to your force field. When your magic is a bit stronger, you might be able to release it without our help."

Jax agreed.

"The Gathering must have originated as an Extraction Spell. The Breaker is obviously very good at them. It actually *could* be part of you in that box."

266

Once they'd left, the central square slowly emptied of its audience. The chattering groups of boys and girls still took a bit of getting used to, compared to the silent segregation when a Gathering had ended.

Benedar said he was going to the Book Rooms. Some of the other Thinkers had already made a start on the newly discovered books, and he was eager to join them.

I realised that I was starving. I hadn't eaten anything yet. Except for that remedy. But magic probably didn't count as food.

Benedar and Alanna stayed to eat with me. He kept giving me sideways glances, until finally I asked him what the matter was.

"Can I...?"

His cheeks were red. Now I was curious. Nothing got Benedar embarrassed.

"Can I touch your magic as well?"

He looked very young all of a sudden.

"Of course," I replied, smiling. "The next time it happens, I'll come and get you."

"There is still the small chance of a link between magic and what's making you sick. But it's very small," he added.

"It's up to you," I said. "I'm not going to *force* you to become a magician."

We laughed. It felt pretty good.

He was about to leave for the Book Rooms,

when Albany appeared. He was running into the square as if he were being chased by a Flyer.

"The Breaker," he said breathlessly. "He's talking properly now, and you won't believe what he's saying."

"What? What is he saying?"

Albany shook his head, as if he still couldn't believe it.

"He's arguing with Groven. And it's about *you*, Cal."

"Me? Why would they be arguing about me?"

"Come and hear it for yourself."

We followed him back to the caves. My thoughts were racing. Was Groven angry that the Breaker had been defeated? Probably. But that wasn't down to me.

All I'd done was help Shannon, unlock the door for Penny, and tell them about the statue.

OK, so it was partly down to me.

But if the Breaker had let Jax and Shannon go free, none of it would have happened. That's what Groven should have been angry about.

Except it wasn't that.

We could hear them shouting before we were ten paces inside the cave entrance.

"Your conceit has been our downfall Varun!"

Groven.

"You were determined to see Callax live as an Exta so you could break him over and over again.

Just to satisfy your *vanity*!"

Groven again.

"I didn't know this would happen. It was a chance in a thousand, a hundred thousand!"

The Breaker. It sounded like he was spitting his words.

"You enjoyed his defeat as much as I did," he went on. "Don't try to deny it."

My defeat? When had I fought the Breaker? Only in my nightmares, but that hardly counted.

"And now the Medaxus enchantment is no more," said Groven. "The magic is gone. And we will die of old age on what remains of this cursed world."

"Are the Exta getting sick yet?" asked the Breaker.

I froze.

"No. Not that I've seen. But they're not magicians anymore, are they? The sickness will take longer this time. There's no magic for it to hold on to."

My thoughts had been racing before, but now they came to a dead stop. I concentrated on breathing, in and out. Alanna and Benedar were staring at me, but I kept my eyes facing forward.

"They will still catch it. The ocean is toxic. They've been eating fish all their lives. Watch the older ones. They will go first."

Now we were all looking at Albany. His face

had gone so white that I could see every single freckle on it. The Breaker's menacing voice continued.

"You know that's why we summon them at eighteen. Any older and they start getting sick. And if they die without a Gathering, all those years unlived are wasted. Uncollected."

"It hardly matters, does it? *There is no more magic.* We gave all we had, to create that spell. It was supposed to last forever. But the House of Medaxus is really gone this time."

This time? I hoped that Benedar was making sense of this, because my head was full of fear, sickness, and death.

And of the terrible memory of putting my face in the ocean the night before. When my shiny new force field had just started to buzz inside my head.

The ocean is toxic. Sickness. Sickness that grabs onto magic. Followed by death.

I spun on my heels and practically ran out of the cave.

I heard the others following me, but I didn't stop. Not until I was back at the ruling house. The closest thing I had to a home.

I was being pretty selfish, really. Albany would be feeling just as bad as me. All I wanted was to lock the door and hide until it all went away.

They didn't let me.

"Cal…"

"Don't touch me, Benedar."

I held my hands up warningly. They started to glow more brightly than I'd ever seen them.

I knew what I was going to do. As quickly as I could, hoping that the magic would stay where I could see it, I returned to the underground room.

I tried not to touch anything on my way. Now that I knew I really was sick, I didn't want to spread it around.

I could hear the others behind me, Albany asking questions and Benedar answering him. I felt a hand on my shoulder, and I flinched away.

"Cal," said Alanna. "I thought we were a team. I've already touched your magic anyway."

"I put my face in the water," I said helplessly. Her eyes widened. "Yesterday. I just wanted to cool down. I didn't know it was toxic."

Another memory presented itself. Garrett holding me under. Breathing ocean water and then throwing it up again when he let me out.

I was in serious trouble.

No wonder all the city's water was filtered twice. We had thought the Opta just wanted to make more work for us. Why else would they bathe in drinking water, after all?

I walked to the white box with my identifier. I put my glowing hands over it, and the underground room disappeared.

* * * * * * * * * * * * * * * * * * * *

I was five. Running through the houses surrounding the central square. No, they were one house. My house. The House of Medaxus.

Something slipped off my head and fell to the stone floor with a clanging noise. I giggled.

"Callax!"

A female voice. Slightly out of breath.

"Your Highness! Please stop!"

I turned. There was an older female looking at me exasperatedly, holding her side. She wore a long brown dress, and her hair was tied back. She bent down to pick up the... crown?

"Sorry, Teela," I said. "I wanted to study, really I did, but my legs wouldn't stay under the table. I tried to make them."

I looked up at her from under my eyelashes. This was a good game.

She smiled.

"Your blue eyes could charm the statue down from the roof, Your Highness. But the king and queen will be looking to me for answers if you don't learn your letters, won't they?"

* * * * * * * * * * * * * * * * * * *

I was seven. Playing hide-and-seek in the

cultivation fields with Teela's daughter. I could see the end of her plait poking out from behind the harvesting machine.

I crept forward carefully. The stalks of the grain crop, newly cut, scratched against my legs. The sun was hot today. I had left the stupid crown behind.

We always counted to a hundred. You could make it out of the city by then, if you ran fast. Otherwise it was too easy.

Wait, I could count to a hundred? No, a thousand. Ten thousand. A million. My head was full of calculations. Facts and figures going on forever.

I was nearly there. Usually Alanna beat me. This was going to be brilliant.

* * * * * * * * * * * * * * * * * * *

I was twelve. About to attend the Academy of Magic for the first time. Except... wasn't this the childstation? No, it was the Academy.

All the books I had read stretched up to the ceiling of my room, shelves and shelves of them. Had I learned enough? The instructors were supposed to be very tough.

All those words I hadn't understood before. I knew them now. Sensibilities. Synapses. Platitudes. Cerebral. Physiology. I knew how to read them, and how to write them down. I could define them.

I felt the reassuring strength of my force field. I was nervous, but as long as I had my magic I knew I would be OK. Here I would just be Cal. I had insisted. No Prince Callax.

It would be hard enough to make friends without *Your Highness*-ing going on all over the place. Protocol be damned.

I still remembered them taking Alanna away.

"You're not compatible, Cal. Your bloodline is different from hers. She will never go to the Academy. Your friendship is pointless."

My father. The king. Stern, handsome, cold. It was rare that I ever pleased him. He expected me to marry a princess from one of the other islands.

I had agreed, if he allowed me normality at the Academy. We had reached an uneasy truce.

* * * * * * * * * * * * * * * * *

I was fourteen. A master magician in training. Garrett, Varun, and I were always trying to outdo each other with new ways of using magic. The Academy pushed us to our limits.

We'd been friends almost from the start. Garrett and I had rescued Varun from a collapsing tunnel. There were many underground passages beneath the city. The Academy filled them with enchantments to test our abilities in the monthly contests.

I was good at creating new spells that would make my island a better place to live. Garrett was good at detection. He read magical energy like the letters on a page.

Varun was best at deconstructing—using magic to remove layers of anything and everything. One at a time. And then putting them back together in new ways.

But there was fear in our lives now. Rumours of a sickness in the rising water. It hadn't reached our island yet. But everyone was worried. Medaxus was only a small part of Imbera. If the other islands fell, so would we.

* * * * * * * * * * * * * * * * * *

I was sixteen. My parents were dead. My sweet mother had held my hand and made me promise to be a just king. Then her eyes had closed and never opened again.

There was almost nothing left for me to rule. The sleeping sickness had worked its way through the population from oldest to youngest.

I knew it wouldn't be long before it reached me. At first, Garrett and I had spent all our time in the Academy's underground workshop. Trying to find a cure. We knew that the sickness was in the water. The stories were true.

Everything from the ocean was filtered twice now, and the rate of new deaths was slowing down. We invented so many different Waking Spells that we lost count.

But people were still getting sick. The time from first sleep to the final death was slower, but it was still happening. We hadn't seen Varun for days. I'd heard that Vita, his older sister, was sick now. He was probably looking after her.

Garrett and I had just travelled the length and breadth of the island to record what was left. I wanted to create some kind of support system for us. If we all put our magic together, we might be able to improve things.

Then we heard that Varun was back in the workshop.

24 The Medaxus Enchantment

The underground room reappeared in front of me, and I lifted my hands from the white box. I staggered to one side, and then my knees gave way completely.

"Fetch the remedy!"

Benedar. Looking after me. I didn't deserve it. I had failed him. I'd failed everyone. The people on this island were my responsibility, and they'd been at the mercy of a madman for two thousand years.

The memories were bright in my head. Still appearing. Surrounding the fragments I had seen before and anchoring them in something real. I was myself again. No more Worker fog.

Now I could make all the links. I kept my eyes closed while the story unfolded. Once I was sure I had remembered everything, I opened them again.

Three worried faces looked down on me.

Benedar held a glass of the remedy. I shook my head. Not yet. Once the sickness really took hold, I would need so much of it. I did not want to waste it by taking some now.

"Sit down," I suggested. "I have a lot to tell you."

"We should go back upstairs," said Benedar.

"No."

I straightened my shoulders and lifted my head.

"No, we'll talk here. This used to be the Academy's workshop. It's important to the story."

I knew that I had spoken differently, with an expectation that they would do as I asked. I couldn't help it.

They all looked at me. The concern on their faces was now mixed with something else. They thought I might really be going crazy this time.

I decided to try something. I was a magician now. I tested my force field. Still weak, still new, but definitely there. And now I knew how to use it.

This room was too cold and white to be pleasant. I created an Illuminator Spell to hover above us. It surrounded our group with a circle of soft, yellow light. The ends of Alanna's hair turned gold, like a sunbeam had touched them. I smiled.

After this, they all sat down without argument. Then I began.

"Two thousand years ago, the world of Imbera was consumed by a progressive sleeping sickness. One by one the islands surrendered to the disease carried by the ocean water. Until only this island prevailed.

"The inhabitants searched for a cure. The sickness discriminated against its victims according to their age, which meant that..."

"Cal!"

Albany looked apologetic.

"I don't understand half of those words."

Benedar's mouth had fallen open in shock. He was more impressed by my vocabulary than my magic, I thought. That was funny.

"Sorry."

I gave a half-shrug and tried again.

"There was a sickness on Imbera. If you caught it, you slept and slept, for longer and longer, until finally you didn't wake up. Older people got sick first. The young magicians who were left tried to find a cure.

"They made spells like that remedy." I pointed to the bottle next to Benedar. "They learned to filter the water. But nothing worked."

"You mean...?"

Benedar looked at me fearfully.

"Yes. I'm going to die."

I smiled, trying to soften my words. "Don't worry. It's not going to happen today. And it's more important that I try to save everyone else. Just listen to the story.

"Varun, who you know as the Breaker, was one of those young magicians. One day his older sister, Vita, got sick. He refused to let her die.

"His special skill had been using magic to deconstruct, to take things apart. Like the Extraction Spell Jax mentioned. Varun learned at the Academy of Magic that used to stand above this room.

"It's the childstation now. But back then it had been where we"—I swallowed the word—"where *they* studied magic.

"He took someone closer to death than his sister. He was desperate enough to try deconstructing what remained of their life so that he could transfer it to Vita.

"It took nearly all his magic, but he did it. He inflicted unimaginable pain on his victim in order to rip their life essence away.

"Then he gave it to his sister. She started to recover. He was jubilant. He tried again. And again.

"So many people were dying already that no one noticed. He perfected his method with Vita's help. Before their magic ran out, he found a way to get more. He discovered that he could separate the force field from the life essence.

"He stored this magic inside the statue that symbolised the ruling house. The creature you know as the Flyer. The statue had enough magical energy of its own to be an excellent guardian.

"Varun thought it rather fitting. He had always envied the royal bloodline, though he had kept this well hidden. He joined the symbols in the stone to the magic in the statue.

"Do you know what those symbols say yet?" I asked Benedar.

He shook his head.

"Not entirely," he replied. "I figured out "House of Medaxus," like I told you, but…"

"They were a promise from the king and queen to their island. The royal family were in charge of the ruling house, but not quite like the Opta."

I tried to think of a way to explain what royalty was. King and queen and prince would all be new words to them.

"Their rule was a privilege granted by birth, but they strived to earn the respect of their people. They worked for the city. They shared its resources."

"And what did their symbols say?" asked Benedar.

"The House of Medaxus. Bound to serve our

ALEX C VICK

people until death, a promise never to be broken," I told him.

"Bound… and broken? Really?" said Alanna.

I nodded.

"He's a common thief," she said furiously. "Everything he has is something that he stole."

"He added the symbols to his arms," I continued. "He created a better spell, a faster spell. Then he decided that he was ready to tell his two best friends.

"One of his friends was the prince of the ruling house. The king and queen were his parents. He was by now the only surviving member of the royal family."

I paused. No one said anything.

"Varun promised his friends eternal life and a cure for the sickness. They refused. The prince argued that living forever was wrong.

"It became clear that the years of extra life would come at the expense of others. And Varun wished to rule. His friends would have to sacrifice their magic to him. They refused again. He… he broke them."

I swallowed. *This* was where all of my nightmares had come from.

"The prince was a powerful magician, and he fought to the last. But Varun had his symbols, and his new spell, and all the magic and lives he had stolen. He won.

"Before he killed the prince, he told him what he was going to do."

I closed my eyes. I could see Varun in front of me. The memory replayed silently in my head.

You are going to live forever, Cal. As my servant. I will find a way. I will give you another life, and then kill you again. And again, and again! The House of Medaxus has a new master!

I opened my eyes.

"Varun showed the prince a white box, a bit like this. It had no panel yet, and no compartments. He told the prince that he would deconstruct him, one layer at a time.

"His magic, Varun would add to the statue. His years of life unlived, Varun would take for himself. The rest would go into the box while he refined his plan."

I paused to see if anyone had figured it out yet. Benedar had tears in his eyes. Albany and Alanna were leaning forward, waiting for me to continue.

"You can see from this room that Varun refined his plan extremely effectively. He had all the time in the world, after all.

"I think that Vita must have contributed to the final Medaxus enchantment and the visions of the Flyers. Spells of Illusion were a speciality of hers.

"Anyone who is now an Opta agreed to sacrifice their magic for protection from the sickness and eternal life. After two thousand years, they have faded until they are more like walking ghosts than people. But they live.

"Anyone who is now an Exta refused. If they were even given the choice at all. Like the prince. They live too. But differently to the Opta. They are not protected from the sickness.

"The parts of them, the *skills* that Varun chooses, are reintroduced to the breeding cycle. They are reborn, over and over, so that the Gatherings can continue. They are allowed no memory of their previous lives.

"But now, it is at an end. The Medaxus enchantment is destroyed. The Opta will die because they are old. The Exta will die because of the sickness. Unless we can find a way to stop it."

I sat back, giving a weary sigh. I couldn't ignore the tiredness anymore. I reached for the remedy, and Benedar handed me the glass that he'd already poured.

His hand was trembling slightly.

I drank it, relieved when the tiredness lifted almost immediately.

The silence went on for what seemed like a long time.

"I'm glad," said Albany. His expression was fierce. "I would rather die knowing who I am, with my freedom returned to me."

Alanna nodded. "Yes. I feel the same. But

there's one thing I don't understand… How do you know so much?"

She stared at me.

"You've got your memories back, obviously, and now you're a Thinker too, but you spoke about it like you were there. When Varun was breaking the prince…"

Her voice trailed off, and I could see the moment that she figured it out.

"He *is* the prince," said Benedar quietly.

"*What?*" said Albany.

"That's why they all know you," said Alanna slowly. "That's why Groven was mad at Varun. You've obviously remembered pieces of this before. During other lifetimes."

She laughed.

"Varun must be beside himself! If he'd only killed you properly the first time, he'd be in charge of Androva by now."

I grinned.

"Yeah. I think I should remind him of that fact, don't you? Now that he's recovered. Now that he knows who I am."

Then I thought for a moment.

"I promised him that I would come for him," I said seriously. "I promised him that he would pay for what he'd done.

"And he *will* pay. But I'm worried about the rest of the Exta. I still have some time. We might be able to stop everyone else from catching the sickness."

Benedar was actually crying now. His small shoulders were shaking.

"Don't," I said to him gently. "Please don't. It will be OK."

I put my hand on his arm, but he shook it off.

"How?" he said angrily. "How will it be OK?"

"Well, for a start, I can get your memories and your other skills back. How about that?

"I don't think we knew each other before, so I can't tell you what your family used to do. But wouldn't it be fun to find out?"

"Can you really?" said Albany enthusiastically. "Can you unlock our boxes too? I thought we'd need to be magicians."

He looked embarrassed.

"And, well, I mean... I'm not sure I want to be a magician if it will make me die more quickly. No offence or anything."

He couldn't look at me.

I laughed.

"No offence taken. And yes, I can unlock the boxes. I remember how to use magic now. It's only a simple Protecting Spell, which is part powered by the cables.

"Like Jax said, he could unlock them too. But the original host for the energy inside needs to be close by. Otherwise it will have nothing to join to. If it's allowed to disperse, it could be lost forever.

"Actually, Varun has done a pretty good job of trapping the sun's energy to augment the magic he had left. This room is a perfect balance of magic and machines."

Albany was already standing beside the box with his identifier on it.

"Now?" I checked.

"Are you kidding?" He nodded. "Of course, now!"

It was easy. He sank to his knees as the memories flooded into his head. We stepped back, giving him some space to figure it all out.

Benedar was next. He was still angry with me, but I persuaded him that finding out about his past would be a better way to spend the next few minutes than shouting at me.

Then it was just me and Alanna. I couldn't read her expression.

"Did you know me?" she asked.

I couldn't lie. She would soon find me out if I did.

"Yes. When we were younger. Your mother was my teacher."

"And when we were older?"

I sighed.

"No. I was told that we would not be compatible. That our friendship had to end."

I waited. I wouldn't blame her if she reacted angrily. She certainly had at the time. She'd screamed at me that I was a despicable, elitist coward, and she never wanted to lay eyes on me again as long as she lived.

To my utter surprise, she smiled.

"I *told* you we weren't compatible," she said, smiling wider. "When we first met, do you remember?"

I nodded.

"I'd quite like the chance to break a few more rules before this is all over," she carried on. Then she went to stand by her white box.

"Show me," she said.

I released the energy.

As soon as she recovered, she marched up to me with a face like thunder. Benedar and Albany hastily got out of her way. She gave me a slap that echoed around the room.

Ouch. It really stung.

"That's for allowing your father to tell you who you can be friends with," she snapped.

Then she gave me a kiss so sweet that it took the sting away.

"What was *that* for?"

"Everything else."

She smiled.

25 Confronting The Breaker

By the time we left the underground room, the sun had disappeared and it was dark again. I was glad the tiredness had not yet returned. The remedy made by the otherworlders was very effective. It would be a while before I had to make any Waking Spells of my own.

I had released the memories and skills of everyone else in our group of ten. It turned out that some of them had known each other before they had first been broken.

Benedar and Haylen had been brother and sister. They were so happy to be together again. Alken had been at the Academy at the same time as me and Garrett, though he had been younger.

There was an awkward moment when he first opened his eyes and saw me.

"Y-your Majesty!" he stammered.

Oh. Yes. I'd become Your Majesty when my father died. Everyone looked at me to see what I would do.

"No," I said firmly.

Alken turned to Albany.

"But he's the *king*!" he said.

"I know," said Albany. "I saw him several times. My family were cultivators before the sickness. Prince Callax used to plant the first seeds of the season."

I remembered the ceremony, although I didn't remember Albany.

"But he's Cal too," Albany went on.

"I'm *just* Cal," I corrected.

Alken didn't look entirely convinced.

"Or Cal-al-al, if you prefer," I said with a grin.

The four of us from my unit started laughing. Benedar tried to explain it to the others, and Alanna gave my hand a squeeze.

"You're not so bad for a king really," she whispered.

We did not remember any of our Exta lives except for the one we were currently living. Our relative ages had shifted around a lot since we had been Imberan.

I supposed that we must all have been the subject of an early binding more than once. If we had always survived the full eighteen years, we would each have been born more than one hundred times by now.

And the chances of *never* upsetting the Opta

during one hundred lifetimes? Nil.

"What do you want to do now?" asked Alanna when we were back upstairs. "Are you... tired?"

There was a shadow on her face as she said this.

"No. Not yet," I said reassuringly.

I needed to speak to Varun. He would know a lot more about the sickness than any of us. It was information that we had to get from him if we were to have any chance of finding a cure.

At the thought of Varun, the fury of my other self burned hot inside my head, just like the Medaxus enchantment. Wanting nothing less than his cries of agony as compensation. Until his life was mine to throw away.

He had ripped me to pieces behind a wall of pain so high that I could not see over the top of it. He deserved to suffer the same fate.

I clenched my fists.

Then I hesitated. Was that really how I wanted to spend the time I had left? Doing to Varun what he had done to me, taking his life in exchange for mine? He'd already lost. He was going to die anyway. It did not need to be at my hand, in cold blood.

But we might be able to use him. I was a magician now, and he wasn't. I knew the spells that would force him to reveal his secrets. I didn't need to torture him, and I wouldn't.

I felt the anger lift. It was a good feeling.

"I need to go to my room," I said. I held up my hand to stop the worried offers of help.

"No, I don't mean because of the sickness. I mean because I want to face Varun tomorrow. Once I have a plan. And I need to practice some spells too."

"Can I watch?" asked Benedar.

"You might be better off reading some of those new books they discovered," I suggested. "The more knowledge we can collect on our own, the better."

He nodded reluctantly. Most of the others decided to go with him. Albany, Alken and Landra were keen to try out their reading skills, now that these had been returned to them.

Which left me, and Alanna, and Orman.

"Do you mind if I stay?" Orman asked.

He shuffled from one foot to the other. His eyebrows were lowered in a proper frown.

"No, I don't mind," I said. "Is there any particular reason?"

"I was older than Vita when it happened," he said. "I saw her get sick, because she lived nearby.

"I don't... I mean, I didn't understand why I wasn't sick first. Well, I had a theory, but..."

"How much older *were* you?" I asked.

"Three years. I'm small for my age. I was then

and I am now."

"*Three years?*" I repeated disbelievingly. "No. That's not possible."

"What was your theory?" asked Alanna. "About why you weren't sick?"

"It's probably nothing," he said, shuffling his feet some more.

"Confidence," I said, raising my hands. The spell reached him almost immediately. He raised his head, and his eyebrows lifted.

"Oh," he said. "My theory is that the water might contain the antidote as well as the poison."

"How?" I asked, smiling. The more I used magic, the more I remembered how much I loved it. Alanna had her hand over her mouth. Her eyes were wide.

"Because I spent more time in the water than anyone I know. And I still didn't get sick."

"Fair enough," I said, lowering my hands.

He blinked.

"I… Can you do that again?" he asked.

"You don't need a spell every time," I told him. "Not really. Remember how it felt. If *you* believe that what you have to say is worth listening to, so will your audience."

"And it was," added Alanna. "It was worth listening to."

He blushed.

"Can you do some more? Spells, I mean."

"Why not? I do need to practice. Especially the Influencing Spells. Varun will probably need plenty of encouragement to talk to us tomorrow."

We had something to eat and then got started.

"Are you sure you want to do this?" I asked. "The spells aren't all positive."

They nodded.

"Alright then."

I raised my hands.

"Fear."

Neither of them liked that one. Orman begged me to stop after only a minute, his eyes dark pools in his face. Alanna's response was to get really, really angry with me.

"Affection."

That was a bit easier. The atmosphere became very friendly, both of them agreeing to do their best to help everyone with everything. They even hugged.

"Love."

I didn't keep that spell up for very long. Orman talked about his younger brother, and Alanna talked about Kaylar. Then she looked at me.

I could see she was trying to fight the spell, but I knew she wouldn't be able to. And if she was ever going to have any feelings for me, I wanted to earn them.

"Amusement," I said hastily.

After a few seconds of confusion, they both started giggling at something. It was hard not to join in. I decided to make that the last spell.

As their laughter faded away, Alanna spoke.

"Do the Love one," she said. "He'll tell you anything."

I raised my eyebrows. "What makes you say that?"

She wouldn't answer me.

We talked about Orman's theory some more. I didn't know how we could put it to the test. I was ashamed to admit it, but I was scared to go near the water again in case the sickness got worse.

Orman went back to his room downstairs, and Alanna joined Kaylar in the room just below mine. There was still no sign of Benedar or the others.

She promised to wake me up the following morning. I felt the tiredness starting to drag me under.

"Don't let me sleep too long," I said. "You'll have to use the remedy to wake me up."

She nodded.

I fell into sleep as if it were a black tunnel that had opened up underneath me. I didn't dream. I didn't wake when Benedar came back. My head was a black pit of nothing.

Then the blackness lifted slightly. I started

choking. I panicked, trying to breathe in, and there was suddenly liquid in my throat, and my nose, and my chest.

I woke up.

"More," said Benedar, holding a small glass to my mouth.

I drank obediently.

The remedy did its job. By the time we were ready to leave, the shadows under my eyes were barely noticeable.

We walked to the caves. The whole group, all ten of us. People stared as we passed them. Talk of Varun's and Groven's argument had spread across the island, if the curious looks were anything to go by.

"Let me go in alone," I said when the caves were in sight. "I know Varun. And you all saw him at the Gatherings. He loves an audience. It will bring out the worst in him."

There was reluctant agreement. Alanna was the only one who refused to wait out of sight.

"Alright," I agreed. "You probably deserve the chance to tell him what you think of him, after what he put you through."

We were early enough that the Opta had not yet begun their work assignments for the day.

Varun tried to cover his shock at seeing me. We took him away from the others.

"Cal…" he said, the familiar smirk of the

Breaker in place.

"No. If you wish to address me, you will call me Your Majesty," I said coldly.

In two seconds, his face went from condescending to enraged.

"*What...?* How...? You..."

He was so angry that he couldn't even speak.

"You can kneel as well," I added, forcing him down with a Movement Spell.

He screamed with rage, his face turning red, but the magic held him and he stayed on his knees. Alanna laughed.

"Oh, Varun," she said. "What did we agree about keeping our composure at all times? This is altogether too *colourful.*"

Having his own words thrown back at him was almost too much. He looked ready to attack us with his bare hands.

I thought he might actually throw off the spell, and I stepped back slightly, pulling Alanna with me. My magic was nowhere near at full strength yet.

He attempted to regain control.

"Magic, Cal?" he sneered. "Really? You know that your death approaches all the faster if you are a magician, don't you?"

"Your Majesty," I reminded him calmly.

"I will *never...*" he started.

"Love," I added, amending the spell.

I trusted Alanna's judgement. She'd told me to use that one. Left to my own devices, I would have chosen Fear.

"Y-your M-majesty," he stammered, and I nearly dropped the spell in shock.

"I want your approval more than anything," he continued. "Please. Please say you forgive me. I've been trying to impress you my whole life."

I swallowed, trying to concentrate. Of all the things I might have expected him to say, it was not this. Asking for my forgiveness? Wanting my approval?

"What have you learned about the sickness since you created this new society?" I asked.

"Almost nothing. The Exta body cannot resist the poison in the water for longer than eighteen years. That is the Gathering age we have settled upon."

"And if they touched the water less? And they didn't eat fish for every meal?" I said.

"That's partly what happens with the Breeders. But it only grants them a maximum of two more years. We don't see the point of it."

Alanna stepped forward again.

"You've *never* tried to find a cure?" she asked incredulously.

"There is no need. It's not as if it is desirable for the Exta to live longer, is it?"

We tried to ask the question in several

different ways, but even though he answered happily enough, he obviously knew nothing that might help us.

Alanna turned to me.

"This is a waste of time. He's not even worth my anger."

"No, he's not. He never was."

I looked back at Varun, holding the spell for one more question.

"Why Opta and Exta?"

He shrugged.

"Optimum is the best, of course. The rest are just Extracts. Pieces and fragments to do with as we wish."

Alanna made a sound of disgust.

I dropped the spell, watching Varun's anger slowly return. Mixed with the embarrassment of remembering what he had told me about wanting my approval, he looked like he was going to explode.

"I will watch you *die*," he said. "And this time you won't be coming back. You're probably already sick, aren't you?

"Yes, I thought there was a chance you might be. What does it feel like to know you've lost? *What does it feel like?*"

"You tell me," I said. I stepped towards him. He held his ground, but his expression flickered. "You could very well die first, Varun. We both know it. You won't get to watch me again. And I will not save you."

I took another step and this time he moved back. I spoke slowly. "But I will not kill you, either. You forget, Varun. I *know* you. Now you must wait for death, humiliated and ignored, working for *me*... It will cause you pain like no other. Consider this my final gift to you."

I smiled. I was free from the Breaker at last. As we left the cave, he screamed in frustration.

26 Near To The End

The others were disappointed that we had not learned anything about how to cure the sickness, but delighted at the thought of the Breaker on his knees.

"Can you do it once more? Just for fun?" asked Albany. "So that we can watch?"

I smiled, shaking my head.

"No. I'm in no rush to see him again."

"Shame," said Albany. "I might have to go and visit him myself. I'll tell him that I'm friends with the king and get him to clean my boots or something."

We spent the next few days revising our plan. Anyone who was due to turn eighteen in the next two weeks was brought to the underground room to have their memories returned.

We didn't think it was fair to let them get sick without any warning. So far I was the only one showing symptoms, but I didn't think that would be the case for too much longer.

However, there was no need to tell the whole island yet. Everyone else deserved to enjoy their freedom for as long as we could protect their ignorance.

The Opta remained surprisingly quiet about it all. Still watching, still waiting, but not actually telling anyone why. I soon realised that the Breaker had not shared the outcome of our little discussion with anyone else. It was obviously too humiliating for him.

It suited me that the rest of the Opta didn't know. I had no desire to discuss the past with them. I was not going to reclaim my outdated birthright, after all.

And I knew who most of them were now. My disappointment at the choice they had made left a bad taste in my mouth. If I thought too much about why they had done it, I might lose my new found peace entirely.

It was getting a little harder for Alanna and Benedar to wake me up every day. But my magic continued to increase in strength. I was someone new now. A combination of Cal the Exta Worker and Prince Callax of the House of Medaxus.

Experimenting with the remedy that the otherworlders had made, I was able to create something more powerful. New spells had always been my speciality, after all.

And we needed it. The first of the older Exta got sick. Then the second, and the third.

I didn't know exactly how long I had left. But no one lived more than a full month after the first sleep of the sickness had taken them. One day I wouldn't wake up.

The otherworlders returned. Just Shannon and Jax this time. Shannon said that Penny was preparing for some kind of test at their Seminary, the Androvan version of the Academy. A school for learning magic. Darius was helping her.

They were full of excitement about their spring celebration. They'd been chosen to represent the Seminary with what they called a special Entertainment Spell. Shannon's face lit up as she described the vision they were going to create.

The more I heard about Androva and Earth, the more my curiosity burned. I wanted nothing more than to see these worlds for myself. I wanted to live a life of discovery, where every day was different from the one before.

But we had all agreed. The otherworlders had saved us once. We could not ask them to take any more risks. Imbera was now on borrowed time. And Shannon and Jax had already been in the water twice.

It was not the same as a lifetime of exposure, but every time they came back, the danger to them would surely increase. It was our battle, not theirs. We had to convince them to stay away—that all was well, and we had no more need of their help.

They had many questions and ideas about the underground room. They were determined to help. They reminded us that Androva had opened a portal to Imbera a long time ago and then turned its back on the horrors it had found.

Shannon noticed that the shadows under my eyes were worse. I made light of it, arguing that it was hard work building a new city.

I distracted them with a demonstration of Influencing Spells. Jax was fascinated. He said that similar spells on Androva were nowhere near as precise, and certainly not taught to underage magicians.

With a mischievous grin, he set about learning as many of them as he could. Shannon, laughing, told me that this was a very bad idea. I taught her the defensive spells. They were both very fast learners.

The time passed quickly, and they were disappointed when they realised they would have to leave.

"We'll come back next week?" Shannon suggested to Jax, and he nodded.

"Don't take this the wrong way," I said, keeping my tone of voice light. "But can you stay away for a while? We have a lot to do, and much as I love learning about your worlds, we need to concentrate on rebuilding our own."

Shannon frowned.

"But we want to help," she argued. "We would have done more this time if we hadn't been trying out new spells…"

Jax looked a bit guilty.

"Yeah, that's my fault. Next time I promise we'll do something a bit more constructive. Sorry."

I shook my head.

"We really appreciate the offer, but we need to do this on our own."

"We do," added Alanna. "We have our pride, after all. We can't rely on you to do everything for us."

She lifted her head and stared at them with perfect confidence. They could not see the fear that was hovering just underneath her determined expression.

"Well… OK," said Shannon hesitantly. "I suppose we could give you some space if that's what you really want."

Jax held her hand, and they had a silent conversation. Her troubled expression lifted, and she nodded.

She turned back to me.

"Let Jax teach you how to open a portal. Then you can come and get us if you need our help."

For a moment I felt dizzy with excitement. Imagine being able to open a doorway to somewhere else whenever I wanted. What if I could walk through it and leave the sickness behind me?

But it was impossible. I would take the sickness with me wherever I went. And I could *never* let Jax and Shannon see how bad it was.

However, I agreed. If they believed that I would use the portal when I needed to, it might be enough to keep them away. To keep them safe.

Jax wrote down the symbols. He gave me three sets of co-ordinates. Two Androvan, and one Terran.

"Terran?" I said.

"It's what Androvans call Earth," said Shannon.

We had a couple of practice runs in the darkness of one of the underground tunnels. It was apparently considered safer to open portals from underground if you had the choice.

The silver shimmer of the portal was like a layer of pure magical energy hanging in the air. It was bittersweet. I was creating the most amazing new magic I had ever learned, knowing all the while that I would not live long enough to use it.

Finally Jax and Shannon were gone. I took a deep breath. My eyes burned with tiredness. It had been difficult to pretend all this time.

Alanna gave me a look of concern, and took hold of my hand. She had only just started to notice the force field buzzing inside her head the day before. Now I could sense the connection flicker between us.

"Do you feel that?" she asked me in amazement.

I pushed my own magic down into the hand that she was holding, as if I were about to project a spell. She breathed in and silver glinted in her eyes.

"I guess you do," she said, her mouth widening in a huge grin.

"Let me take some more Waking Remedy, and then you can try a few basic spells," I suggested.

Time passed. I spent most of my time stockpiling Waking Spells, so that there would be enough for as many Imberans as possible. I taught Alanna how to make them too.

We were careful not to create any more magicians. I folded the papers with the portal instructions and locked them away. Without a live force field, no one would be able to use them, but I didn't want to take any chances.

We discovered more books, and more about the history of our world and its islands. There were many legends about the ten kings and queens who had first inhabited them.

My days inevitably got shorter. To my relief, Alanna showed no signs of getting sick. It seemed that as long as she stayed away from the ocean, she was young enough to stay well. For now at least.

Then something unexpected happened. Or rather, didn't happen. One of the older Exta didn't get sick. Not at all. And he had worked in an ocean unit.

I was the first to notice the coincidence. I had to spend more and more time lying in bed, and the others in our group had taken to producing written reports. I could read them at my own pace and still keep up with what was going on.

Orman's theory! We had abandoned it as an idea, unable to come up with a link that would help us. But this was surely proof that there was something protective in the water alongside the poison.

Except the only way to find out was to go into the water. And I would not ask anyone to do that. Not when we didn't know what we were looking for. When it could cause them more harm than good.

It would have to be me. And I would have to do it quickly, before I lost the strength to get out of bed. And before Alanna realised and tried to stop me. Or worse, went into the water herself.

I questioned Orman and the other Exta, trying

to make my interest sound casual. I told Orman I just wanted a complete picture of his life before the sickness. I said I was doing it for everyone.

But there was little common ground in their answers. Then Orman mentioned something almost as an afterthought.

"I did cut myself that one time," he said.

"When? Where?" I said, pushing back the exhaustion.

"It was where you said you touched the Flyer, actually," he said. "On the edge of the island. Those rocks are even more jagged under the surface than they are on top of it."

He laughed self-consciously.

"I was convinced I'd found the magical rocks. You know what people used to say about where the statue of the Flyer came from?"

He rolled his eyes.

"My parents were so angry. I got my foot stuck when I swam too far down. I nearly ran out of air. I just wanted to see if the rocks would glow for me. And then somehow I got my foot out."

He showed me a mark just above his toes. It was a scar in the shape of a small crescent.

"It took forever to heal," he went on. "And I still have it, all these lives later. I suppose the water really was poisoned, even then."

"I suppose…" I said absently.

Something was niggling at my memory about those rocks. Something important. But I was too tired to figure it out just then.

The following day, when I lifted my eyelids, Benedar's face was terrified.

"What?" I said groggily, rubbing my eyes. They always felt like they were full of rock dust now.

"Do you know how long it took me to wake you up this time?" he asked.

Before I could answer, his eyes filled with tears.

"A long time?" I guessed.

"I thought you were dead."

"Oh. Well… that's not good."

I sighed.

"It's going to happen," I said softly. "I thought you knew that."

He shook his head.

"If you hadn't become a magician, you might have had a chance!" he burst out angrily.

"You don't know that," I said.

"Albany isn't sick yet, did *you* know *that*?"

"What?"

"He was eighteen last week."

"He…"

Suddenly my head lit up with the connection.

"Get him!" I said. "I need to ask him something. And then get that history book about the royal houses. The one you found last week. I need the bit about the statue of the Flyer."

.

27 An Ending And A Beginning

Benedar ran off to do as I'd asked. One of the benefits of being this ill was that everyone wanted to keep me happy.

I drank some more Waking Remedy. It didn't make me feel much better. I had the feeling I could drink the whole bottle now, and not wake up properly.

I needed to concentrate. I was nearly out of time.

Alanna came to sit with me, her face anxious. We didn't speak.

As soon as Albany appeared, I asked him to show me his arm.

"What? My arm?" he said in confusion. He lifted his sleeve.

"No," I said. "The other arm. The one you cut on the rocks that time."

He showed me. When I saw the crescent shaped scar, I could have shouted with relief, if only I'd had the energy to do it.

"What does it mean?" he asked. "It didn't heal for a long time…"

I shook my head slowly, trying to focus. I could see the fear on his face.

"The other Exta, from the ocean unit…"

I searched my mind for his name.

"Axton. Can you find him? He might have the same kind of scar. Come back and tell me?"

He nodded, and disappeared.

Alanna linked her fingers together with mine. I felt a tear drop onto the back of my hand.

Then Benedar came back with the book I'd asked for.

"The… statue. How did they make it?"

Benedar turned the pages.

"It's more of a legend than real history. A story for children. That the island of Medaxus has always had the Flyer to protect it.

"The first queen claimed that the statue was carved from magical rocks. They're supposed to glow when someone of royal blood is nearby.

"But no one knows which rocks. And there is no more magic in the statue of the Flyer now."

I looked at Alanna. My eyelids were so heavy.

"Y-your mother, she taught me. I think. The rocks where Albany cut himself. And Orman. And Ax…"

She held a glass to my lips, and I tried to

swallow, I really did, but it was so hard.

I could hear urgent voices. Scrambling footsteps. Then shouting. Then nothing.

I was drifting. Floating. Or being carried? I didn't know.

It was dark. The stars seemed bigger. Was I outside? My breathing was getting slower.

"Keep your eyes open, keep your eyes open, *keep your eyes open!*"

Was that request for me? I was disappointed. I really wanted to close my eyes.

Suddenly, my eyes opened wide. There was a line of fire along the inside of my left arm. The pain was sharp, making me gasp.

"Should we do the other arm? He's really bleeding."

"I don't know. *I don't know!*"

The pain faded. I closed my eyes.

* * * * * * * * * * * * * * * * * *

I was so thirsty. I didn't expect to feel so thirsty when I was dead. Everything hurt. But especially my arm.

"He *is* breathing. As long as he's breathing, he's alive."

I knew that voice. Benedar?

"It's been ages. Shouldn't he have woken up by now?"

Alanna. I wanted to show that I could hear her. I tried to move, but nothing happened. I slept.

The next thing I felt was a hand resting briefly on my arm. It made the pain worse and better at the same time. Then I was aware of cold water, and a cloth.

The pain burned, and I felt my chest heave to take in air. Suddenly I was breathing faster, louder, and my eyelids were lifting.

"Benedar!"

The sound of running footsteps.

It was bright. I winced. The light immediately reduced.

"Cal…"

A whisper. Alanna's face, Benedar's face. Blurred. My tears or theirs? I didn't know. I hadn't thought to see them again. I was grateful for the chance to say goodbye properly.

"A-am…" I coughed. "Am I still alive? Can I have a glass of the…?"

Cold liquid trickled down my throat.

"How do you feel?" asked Benedar.

They both looked at me nervously.

I blinked. I felt different. Then I realised what it was. I didn't feel tired. But how could that be? I'd only drunk a tiny amount of Waking Remedy.

I struggled to sit, grimacing when I tried to use my left arm to push myself upwards.

"Cal? How do you feel?"

"Better than I usually do. Despite the fact that I seem to have done something to my arm."

I shifted until I was sitting straighter. I was starting to feel restless. It was a strange feeling. I wanted to run down the stairs and *do* something.

"I feel… great," I said. "I'm starving, actually. Did you make a new kind of Waking Remedy?" I said to Alanna.

"Don't you remember?" said Benedar. "The rocks, the statue, Albany's scar? The same as Orman's and Axton's…"

All of a sudden, I *did* remember.

"You don't mean it worked?" I said incredulously.

"It looks like it," said Benedar, grinning.

I stared down at my arm. It was a bit of a mess, but the skin was already starting to form a crescent shape around the edges.

I laughed in amazement. I hugged Benedar and then Alanna. I held onto her for a long time. Our force fields lit up at the connection, and her eyes were like silver stars when I finally drew back.

"We have to protect everyone," I said, starting to get up. "The others who were sick. We have to…"

Alanna pushed me back.

"You have time to eat." She smiled. "We've

already started looking after the others. No one is going to die, Cal. Not now."

The next few days sped by. Alanna and I created a spell to unlock the power within the rocks so that we could protect the rest of the population more quickly.

The same scar appeared on everyone, even when the cure was administered by magical means.

"It looks like a tooth, or maybe a claw," said Alanna. "You know, from the Flyer?"

Mine was the biggest, even after I used Healing Spells to try to reduce the size of the wound.

Benedar apologised, saying that they had been so desperate to save me, they hadn't cared about the damage they might be doing. I reassured him. I didn't mind at all.

"Did they glow?" I asked him curiously. "The rocks?"

"We didn't see anything at first," said Alanna. "But Albany was the one who noticed it. It was deep underneath the water."

I nodded. I remembered. I'd seen a glow when Garrett was holding me under the water all those years ago. I'd thought the lack of air was causing me to imagine it.

"There was some magic left on the island after all," I said. "It is fortunate that the Opta never knew about it."

We were creating new magicians now. Once the memories had been returned, everyone wanted their magical ability back too.

One day the Opta started ageing. Slowly at first, and then faster and faster. Then they began to die.

I was glad. They did not deserve to live, but I had not wanted us to become murderers. My friends deserved a future free from any regrets. As our island rebalanced itself, a new optimism took hold.

Finally, it was the Breaker's turn. I refused to see him, but he asked for me so many times that I relented.

"Cal," he said. His voice cracked. His eyes were sunken and afraid. His skin was like ancient paper, crisscrossed with lines of old age and pain. The Breaker, broken.

"Varun."

"I heard that you found a way to cure it."

"Yes."

"The House of Medaxus rises again," he said.

"No. There is no royal family anymore. The future is unwritten."

"I wish… I wish I had chosen differently. But I cannot change who I was."

"No," I said again. "The past is the past."

"There is one thing," he offered.

"What?"

"He is alive, of course. They all are."

I tilted my head suspiciously.

"Garrett."

I inhaled sharply. The hope was almost too great to fit inside me. Then I understood.

Of course. After every Gathering, the lives were sent back. Garrett would be... what? Three years old? But he'd be alive.

I exhaled again. Talik. Dervan. Jory. Zack. Dane. They all lived.

The Breaker looked at me. I nodded. It was enough. He closed his eyes as I turned my back on him for the last time.

There were wings on my feet as I ran to the childstation. I searched for Vella, the only person I really knew.

She asked me to slow down. I was talking so fast that the words were jumbling together.

She said she knew a Garrett, and asked me to follow her. We went to one of the newly designated playrooms. She pointed to one of the boys with his back to us.

As I watched, he turned slightly, and his profile, so familiar even in miniature, made me catch my breath. His messy hair was the same yellow colour that I remembered.

I could feel sudden tears forming. They stung my eyes and made me blink. Why was I crying when I should be happy?

He was frowning with concentration as he stacked coloured rocks on top of each other.

"Garrett…" said Vella softly.

He looked up.

"There's someone to see you," she said.

I walked over to him and knelt down.

"Who are you?" he said.

"I'm Cal," I replied.

"Do I know you?" His frown deepened. His grey eyes were direct and unafraid.

"Not yet," I said. "But I'd like to be your friend, if you'll let me. And when you're a bit older, there's a story I'd like to tell you."

"What kind of story?" he said curiously.

"An adventure. With magic and spells and good and evil. I can show you it all happening inside your head until it will be part of you."

He considered this.

"Alright, Cal. That sounds like fun. Do you want to help me build this tower?"

"Yes." I nodded. "Yes. There's nothing I'd like more."

When I explained it to the others later, they could hardly believe it. Not because they didn't want to, but because, like me, they thought it was too good to be true at first.

Benedar was annoyed with himself for not making the link before. Alken went to look for

Dervan straight away.

In fact, everyone who was now an older brother or sister wanted to find the children who had once been *their* older brothers and sisters.

Alanna asked me to go with her so that I could meet the girl who had taught her how to survive the ruling house.

"Without Antia, I wouldn't have lasted five days," she admitted. "It broke my heart when she left. I nearly couldn't build a wall big enough to hide the grief behind."

"Do you still do that?" I asked her. "Build walls, I mean?"

She lowered her gaze.

"Not really. Except when I thought you were dead."

Then she looked at me.

"When you did that Influencing Spell, the Love one, they all came crashing down," she told me.

"Every last one. That's how I knew that Varun wouldn't be able to resist it. It was terrifying. I would have told you whatever you wanted to know."

When we reached the childstation, we found the small Antia playing with Garrett. We joined them. Garrett was delighted to see me back again so soon.

A few days later, it was finally starting to feel

as if things might be settling down. The Opta were gone forever and we were free. But there was still one thing left to do.

"I want to try something," I said to Alanna. "Something new."

"Something new?" she asked. "Are you kidding? Haven't we had enough change to be going on with for a while?"

"This is a good thing," I promised.

I took her to the underground tunnel, and she protested, saying that the sun was out, and she didn't want to spend any time below the surface.

I leaned in to kiss her while she was still talking, and after a moment she kissed me back. Our force fields lit up the darkness, and I felt invincible. We were alive. We were together. I would never take it for granted.

When I took the papers out of my pocket, she recognised them straight away. She smiled. I started to lay them out on the rocky floor, but she picked them up and held them open in front of me.

I drew the magical energy onto the walls next to us. Finally, I completed the sequence and entered the coordinates.

"We should say thank you properly," I said. "And I am kind of curious. Aren't you?"

The shimmering doorway to Androva rose up in front of us, and we stepped forward. It was time to start writing our future.

The Legacy of Androva Series
(To Be Continued...)

Stealing Magic
Capturing Magic
Seeking Magic
Controlling Magic
Breaking Magic

You can find out more about the author, and the rest of
the books in the Legacy of Androva series, at
www.alexcvick.com

Made in the USA
Coppell, TX
21 July 2022